THE NEVER ENDING BIRTHDAY

Katie Dale

MACMILLAN
CHILDREN'S
BOOKS

First published 2017 by Macmillan Children's Books
an imprint of Pan Macmillan
20 New Wharf Road, London N1 9RR
Associated companies throughout the world
www.panmacmillan.com

ISBN 978-1-5098-1072-7

1 3 5 7 9 8 6 4 2

A CIP catalogue record for this book is available from
the British Library.

Printed and bound by CPI Group (UK) Ltd, Croydon CR0 4YY

For my wonderful Dad.
Thank you for everything, especially for
always being there for me, time after time . . .

DAY 1

MAX

The moment I wake up, the salty smell of bacon fills my nose, and my eyes fly open, excitement zipping through my veins like electricity. Mum only makes us bacon butties in bed on special occasions, and today's special because . . . it's our *birthday*! WOO-HOO!

My feet twitch, my stomach rumbles and every inch of me itches to run downstairs, but I force myself to stay put, waiting for Mum and Dad to burst through my bedroom door with a chorus of 'Happy Birthday' like they do every year.

Suddenly I hear footsteps on the stairs – *this is it*! I pull my duvet up to my chin, screw my eyes shut tight and even snore a little for effect. *Three . . . two . . . one . . .*

Nothing.

I open one eye. Then two.

Then the smoke alarm goes off.

Uh-oh.

ANNI

The screeching alarm jolts me awake like an electric shock.

Omigosh! Is the house on fire? My heart hammers as

1

I scramble out of bed and hurry downstairs, fire-safety instructions streaming through my head. *Get outside as quickly and safely as possible, do not take your possessions, do not stop, do not panic.*

How are you meant to NOT panic? We could all die in a blazing inferno! My pulse quickens, and – I can't help it – I break into a run, desperate to get to the front door, to safety, when suddenly I trip – 'Oof!'

'Anni!' Mum cries, hurrying over. 'Are you OK?'

'We have to get out! There's a fire!' I cry, jumping up.

'No, darling, it's just your dad burning breakfast.' She sighs, standing on tiptoe and flapping a tea towel at the incessant alarm. 'Max! What have I told you about leaving your football kit in the middle of the floor?'

'That Anni'll be bound to trip over it?' Max smirks, ambling downstairs. 'Why can't you just look where you're going for once, Anni?'

'Well why can't *you* just put things away for once?' I retort.

'It's not my fault you got all the clumsy genes!'

'I'm *not* clumsy!' My cheeks burn. 'Besides, it's better than . . . than getting all the *stupid* genes!'

Max scowls. 'Better than—'

'Twins, please!' Mum cries, finally swatting the smoke alarm into silent submission. 'Not today. It's your birthday!'

Our birthday? I'd almost forgotten! I'm thirteen at last. A teenager!

'Come on, let's have breakfast,' Mum says with a smile, wrapping her arms around us and leading us into the smoky kitchen.

'Happy birthday!' Dad cries, turning, red-faced, from the hob, brandishing a sizzling frying pan. 'You like your bacon crispy, right?'

My stomach lurches as Dad scoops the shrivelled black curls on to a slice of bread, but he looks so hopeful I force a smile. 'Yum!'

MAX

Yum? Seriously?

'Er, there's crispy, then there's *cremated*!' I laugh, pushing my plate away as I join Anni and Mum at the kitchen table. 'No thanks!'

'Max! Don't be so rude!' Anni chides, biting into her sandwich. 'It's delicious!'

CRUNCH!

I wince. She'll be lucky if she hasn't broken a tooth! Serves her right. Goody-two-shoes Anni is always making me look bad in front of Mum and Dad, but there's being polite, then there's getting food poisoning, and I can't risk *that* – not today of all days!

'Mu-um,' I wheedle. '*Please* can you cook some more?

3

You know just how I like it – pink and floppy. And it is my birthday . . .'

'I'm sorry, love, there's no more bacon. How about cornflakes instead?' she suggests.

'Er . . . I used the last of the milk in my coffee,' Dad says guiltily. 'Sorry.'

'I'll just have toast.' I sigh.

'Actually . . . we're out of bread too,' he confesses.

'But . . . it's the Cup Final today!' I cry. 'I need my strength!'

'So stop being a princess, and eat your bacon butty like everyone else,' Anni scolds.

'You mean like you and Dad,' I correct her. '*Mum's* not eating one either.'

'Oh I . . . um . . . already ate,' Mum says, glancing at Dad, her freckled cheeks growing as pink as Anni's do when she fibs. Case closed.

'Present time!' Dad cries, rushing into the hall and returning with two brightly wrapped parcels. 'One each now, and the rest this evening.'

I grin as he hands me a shoebox-shaped present. YES! It's the designer football boots I've spent months begging for! Now there'll be no stopping my goal-scoring skills in today's match!

I tear through the paper at record speed, but – *no!*

'What's the matter, Max?' Mum frowns. 'Are they the wrong size?'

'No . . . they're the wrong *boots*!'

'They look the same to me,' Dad says, peering over my shoulder. 'Same colour . . .'

'But they're not the right brand!' I point at the logo. 'I've never even *heard* of this make.'

'Brand names are for pretentious idiots!' Dad sniffs, folding his arms over his round belly. 'These were half the price of the designer boots you showed me, and the reviews are just as good.'

'But . . .'

'Honestly, Max, they're just boots!' Anni scoffs. 'Who cares what brand you wear as long as you play well?'

Grr. 'The right boots will *help* me play well!' I explain.

'A bad workman blames his tools!' she trills.

'Oh *shut up*, Anni!' I yell, slamming the box down on the table. 'Like you know anything about football boots! Or *any* sport, come to that!'

'Max! Anni! *Please!*' Mum scolds, running her hands through her frazzled blonde hair. 'What Anni means is you don't need special boots to play well, love. You're a brilliant footballer. Why don't you try them on? Have a kick-around.'

'But then you won't be able to return them!'

'Max!' Anni gasps. 'Don't be such a spoilt brat!'

I scowl at her, my insides churning. I don't mean to sound ungrateful, it's just . . . I had my heart set on those boots – I've been dreaming about them for months – and today

5

they could make all the difference in the Cup Final . . .

'No. Max is right,' Dad says tightly. 'If he doesn't want these boots, I'll return them.' He picks up the box.

'Really? Thanks, Dad!'

'But you're not getting any replacements.'

'What?' I stare at him. 'But Dad! That's so *unfair*!'

'*Case closed!*' Dad thunders, shoving the shoebox into a cupboard and slamming the door.

ANNI

Way to spoil our birthday, Max.

I glare at him as he slumps in his chair, arms folded, like a toddler having a tantrum. He's so immature! You'd never believe he's thirteen. Or my twin.

Dad takes a deep breath, trying to calm down. 'Anni, sweetheart, why don't you open your present?'

I carefully unwrap the pretty silver wrapping paper and pull out a top. At least, I think it's a top. It's nearly long enough to be a dress, and baggy enough to fit about three of me! And it's pink. Bright, Barbie-doll pink. I NEVER wear pink.

Max snorts.

'Do say if you don't like it, won't you, Anni?' Mum says anxiously. 'I wasn't sure, but the shop assistant said that style's very "in" at the moment, and—'

'It's lovely!' I insist, forcing a smile as I jump up to

kiss them both. There's no way I can let Mum and Dad see how much I hate it, especially after Max's outburst. 'I love it! Thank you so much!'

'You're welcome.' Dad smiles and kisses my cheek. 'Happy birthday! I'm really sorry, I have to work late again tonight, but—'

'What?' Max's head snaps up. 'You're still coming to my match, though, right?'

'I'm sorry, mate—'

'But it's the Cup Final!' Max protests. 'Is it because I didn't like the boots? I'm really, really sorry!'

'No, it's nothing to do with that.' Dad sighs. 'You know I'd be there if I could, but I have to work and—'

'You *always* have to work,' Max mutters bitterly, kicking the table.

'Max!' Mum chides.

'I'll make it up to you,' Dad promises. 'Why don't you both invite some friends over for a birthday tea?'

'That's not the same,' Max grumbles.

'Well . . . I'm sorry, there's nothing I can do.' Dad shrugs wearily, picking up his jacket. 'I've got to go.'

'Can you film it for him, Mum?' Max asks as Dad hurries out. 'Then we can all watch it together afterwards?'

Mum winces. 'Actually . . . I'm really sorry, but something's come up and—'

'*You're* not coming *either*?' Max exclaims, horrified.

'I'm so sorry, love. It's just this once. I'll be back by six thirty—'

'I don't *believe* it!' Max jumps up, knocking his chair over with a loud clatter. '*Neither* of you are coming? To the biggest match of the *season*? On my *birthday*?' He storms out of the kitchen.

'Max, wait!' Mum hurries after him.

I roll my eyes, take another bite of my sandwich, then realize no one's watching, and dump the rest in the bin. *Yuck!*

MAX

'Hey, Max, wait up!' Ben cries, running over and leaping on to my shoulders as I cut across the village green.

'Get off!' I grumble, shrugging him off.

'Cheer up, mate!' Ben grins. 'I got you a prezzie! Sorry, I didn't have time to wrap it.' He pulls a king-size chocolate bar from his bag. 'Happy birthday!'

'Thanks, Ben!' Maybe things are looking up! I rip the wrapper and hungrily tuck in.

'Easy – you don't want to get stomach ache before the big match.' Ben laughs. 'Did you get those football boots you wanted?'

My smile slips. 'No. Dad got the wrong ones.'

'Oh no!'

'*And* they're not even coming to watch.'

'What a shame.' Ben frowns. 'Actually, Max I wanted to ask you—'

'Heads up!'

Out of nowhere, a football smacks into the side of my head, knocking me sprawling into the mud. 'OUCH!'

'Sorry, mate!' I look up and recognize Jake Kane, Farlington School's goalie, jogging over. 'You're gonna need better reflexes than that to beat us in the Cup Final! Hope I haven't bruised that pretty ickle face of yours? You're a delicate lot at Bridgehill, aren't you?'

I scowl at him. *Delicate?* I'll give him *delicate*! I jump to my feet, grab the ball and hurl it back at him as hard as I can, but he sidesteps suddenly and the ball whizzes straight past – smashing the window of a nearby house.

Uh-oh.

Ben gasps.

The front door flies open and an old lady totters out, wiping her hands on a tea towel.

'Who did that?' she yells, glaring at us.

Jake immediately points at me, and my cheeks grow hot.

'I'm sorry. It was an accident!' I insist.

'Flipping kids!' she snaps. 'What's your name?'

'Max Sanchez,' Jake yells. 'He goes to Bridgehill School.'

I glare at him.

'Well, you'll be paying for that window, Max Sanchez, make no mistake!'

I sigh. Today just keeps getting better and better.

ANNI

I check my watch for the millionth time as I wait on Belle's chilly garden wall. We're going to be late if she doesn't hurry up, but she's warned me not to ring her doorbell. She *says* it gives her mum a headache, but we've been friends for three months now, ever since I moved here, and I haven't been inside her house once. She always wants to hang out at mine instead. I can't help feeling that maybe she's a bit embarrassed by me. I shiver and pull my coat tighter. Even on a sunny day it's so much colder up here than in London.

Suddenly Belle storms out of her house, marches down the driveway – and straight past me!

'Belle? Are you OK?' I ask, hurrying after her.

'Don't ask,' she mutters, hugging her arms tightly.

OK.

Belle's not exactly a morning person – but I know it's nothing personal. Sometimes her moods last all day and sometimes they blow over in minutes. But even when she's angry, she's one of the prettiest girls I've ever seen, her cheeks flushed, flame-red curls springing in all directions, her grass-green eyes burning with hazel flecks.

She looks at me. 'What have you done to your hair?'

'Do you like it?' I smile, my hands flying to the fishtail

plait I'd spent ages on this morning, determined to look sophisticated now I'm thirteen.

Belle shrugs. 'I prefer it loose.'

'Oh.' I pull my hairband off and begin unwinding the strands.

'Here, I'll help. After all, it's your first day of being a teenager – you need to look the part. Happy birthday, by the way.'

'Thanks!' I beam. She remembered! I wasn't sure she would. She's sometimes a bit forgetful. She often leaves stuff at home, but I'm always happy to lend her my things. Speaking of which . . .

'Have you finished with my mobile yet, Belle? Only Mum's been asking—'

'Sorry, I forgot – it's in my room.'

'Right . . .' I glance back at her house. It's literally steps away.

'Come on, we're running late – I'll bring it round after school if you like? Or do you have birthday plans?'

'Actually Mum's cooking a birthday dinner and Dad said we could invite some friends.' I smile. 'Would you like to come?'

'Course!' Belle grins. 'Straight after school?'

'No, Max has a football match and Mum and Dad have to work late, so it'll be about six thirty.'

'Wait.' Belle stops walking. 'So your house will be

empty for three and a half hours?'

'Well . . . yes.'

Her eyes light up. 'Awesome! Party time!'

I falter. 'Oh, well, I'm not sure . . .'

'Anni, it's your birthday! You're thirteen! You *have* to have a party!'

My skin tingles with excitement. But . . . I can't throw a party without asking Mum and Dad, can I? I bite my lip, thinking fast. They *are* always encouraging me to make more friends, and they *did* say we could invite a few people round for dinner – they'd just be getting there a bit early, that's all . . .

'But it's such short notice – won't people have to get home?'

Belle shakes her head. 'Not *everyone* has a straight-home-from-school curfew, you know!'

'But who would I even invite? I don't really know many people at school.'

'Exactly! This is the perfect way for you to *get* to know people!' Belle insists. 'After all, they'd *have* to talk to you at your own party, right?'

My heart swells with hope. I'd love to make more friends. It's been so difficult since we moved to Yorkshire after Christmas. For me at least. Max's football skills and loud mouth soon scored him a whole gang of mates, but it's harder for me, especially as everyone else was already in friendship groups.

I still have nightmares about my first day here. I felt so alone, so homesick, especially when I walked through the canteen at lunchtime. I didn't know anyone, had no idea where to sit, and then when I finally spotted a free chair next to a girl from my class, she hastily shoved her bag on to it and I almost burst into tears. I might've done, if it hadn't been for Belle.

'But – but what if no one comes?' I ask anxiously now. How mortifying would that be? 'Besides, we haven't got time to go shopping for food and drink or anything –'

'Anni, you silly bean, of *course* people will come!' Belle laughs. 'And all we need is a house and a stereo. I'll sort the tunes, the invites – everything. My mum is the *queen* of parties – she throws them all the time! Leave everything to me.'

'But—'

'Anni, sweetie, stop worrying!' She cups my face in her hands and I stare into her gleaming green eyes. 'You *need* this party. You *deserve* this party. How else are people going to discover what a sweet, thoughtful, kind, lovely person you are?'

A rush of warmth floods through me. She really thinks I'm all those things? I still can't believe my luck at being befriended by bright, beautiful, blazing Belle that first lunchtime. I'll never understand why she picked me to sit next to her and be her BFF, and I'll never be able to repay her. Or maybe I can . . .

'*Please* have a party, Anni!' she begs. 'Please, please, *please*, with a cherry on top and whipped cream and chocolate sauce and hundreds and thousands and—'

'OK!' I giggle. 'But only invite a few people!'

'YES!' Belle squeals, grabbing my hands and jumping up and down. 'You're the best best friend in the entire WORLD!'

I beam. Maybe this birthday is going to turn out well after all.

MAX

This is the worst birthday ever.

a) I got the wrong present and had no (edible) breakfast.
b) I broke a window (and it wasn't even my fault!), then had to spend twenty minutes sweeping up the broken glass while grumpy Mrs MacCready yabbered on and on about 'young people these days'.
c) I finally got to school only to discover the old crone's *already* called and doomed me to lunchtime detention even though Ben ran ahead and tried to explain what had happened!
d) We've got our Year 8 maths test first thing, which, of course, I forgot to revise for.

Terrific.

I slump down at a table near the back of the classroom.

Then I grit my teeth. The world may be out to get me, but this is *my* birthday and I'm not going down without a fight! Time for a Max Sanchez Oscar-winning performance!

I clutch my stomach and stick my hand up in the air. '*Miss!*'

'Yes, Max?' Ms Ford says.

'Miss, I – I don't feel very well!' I moan, pulling my best *I'm dying* face.

She looks concerned, just as expected.

But then Ben opens his big mouth.

'Oh no! Was it that king-size chocolate bar I gave you?' he says anxiously. 'I warned you it could give you stomach ache!'

I glare at him.

'Dear me, chocolatitis, is it?' Ms Ford raises an eyebrow. 'Carameasles? Or PAIN au chocolat?'

A giggle spreads round the room and I scowl. Her jokes are so pathetic. If I wasn't supposed to be ill, I could top them all by saying I'm *Sickers*.

'No, miss, I really don't feel well – I think I might throw up!' I clap my hand over my mouth and make a retching noise so convincing that several girls nearby squeal and jump out of their chairs.

Awesome.

'Oh dear.' Ms Ford frowns. 'In that case, you'd better come with me.'

Result! I grab my bag, clutching my stomach as I head for the door – no test for me!

But suddenly she pulls out a chair at the front.

'You can sit here. That way I'll be on hand if you feel unwell.'

'What?' I blink. 'But –'

'Here.' She passes me the waste-paper bin. 'Just in case.'

'But, miss . . . !'

'Max, the only "but" I want from you is *your* butt on *that* chair. Now.'

I slump down, defeated.

Pants.

ANNI

'Omigosh, that test was so HARD!' I moan to Belle as we head outside at break-time. 'I couldn't even *understand* some of the questions, let alone *answer* them, and we're in top set!' I hate to think what score Max got – he didn't even revise.

'It wasn't that bad.' Belle shrugs.

I frown. 'What mark did you get?' Our teacher deliberately mixed up our test sheets before she handed them round for us to mark.

'A hundred.'

Full marks? I only got seventy-two!

'I could come round and help you study at the weekend if you like?' Belle offers. 'Maybe even sleep over? Mum's having one of her parties, so I'll be super-bored at home anyway.'

'Thanks,' I say. *But that won't change my results . . .* What if everyone else in top set got full marks? What if I get moved down – away from Belle? Mum and Dad will be SO disappointed in me! Why oh *why* didn't I revise *harder*? I'm so worried about it, I don't pay attention in my next lesson and get two answers wrong. I'm going to get moved down in *all* my classes if I'm not careful, and that would be a complete and utter *disaster*!

'Stop frowning, Anni – it'll give you wrinkles,' Belle chides as we join the lunch queue. 'You've gotta look after your skin now you're a teenager, you know. In fact . . .' She squints at my face. 'Is that a little spot?'

'What?' I gasp, horrified. 'Where?'

'Just by your nose.'

My hand flies to my face.

'Don't touch it!' Belle tuts. 'You'll make it worse.'

'Sorry!' I swear I can now feel the spot throbbing on my face. Omigosh, can everyone else see it too? It feels like Vesuvius about to erupt!

'Don't worry, I've got my make-up in my bag – I'll fix it after lunch.' She eyes the counter as the queue moves forward. 'Hmm, vegetable lasagne or chicken salad. No contest. Salad, please!' she tells the dinner lady.

'Um, same please,' I say distractedly.

'Anni . . .' Belle sighs. 'You're such a sheep.'

I blink. 'What?'

'You don't have to have the same as me every day, you know? Make your own decisions.'

'OK – lasagne, please.'

'Are you only having that now because I told you to?' Belle raises an eyebrow.

'Lasagne or salad?' the dinner lady asks impatiently.

'Um . . . I . . .' I stare at her, flustered. *Which should I choose?* If I go for salad, I'm copying Belle, and if I choose lasagne she'll think I'm just doing what she told me to!

'Salad, then,' the dinner lady says briskly, passing me a bowl of limp lettuce and shrivelled chicken.

Belle shakes her head. 'Anni, Anni, Anni.'

I stare miserably at my plate as I follow Belle towards the tables. After my horrible half-breakfast, I could really do with lasagne. What kind of idiot can't even choose their own lunch? No wonder Belle's embarrassed by me.

'Hey, guys!' she cries as we pass a table of Year 9s. 'Party at Anni's house after school! Thirty-three, Elm Road – four o'clock! Be there or be square!'

What? 'Belle!' I hiss, once we're out of earshot.

'Do you even know them?'

'Not yet.' She grins. 'But if we get in with super-hot Idris and his crowd, we'll be instantly popular!'

'Idris?' I glance back at the table. Several of the guys are good-looking, but one is so gorgeous he looks like he just stepped straight off a movie set. He has a lovely kind smile, and eyes as blue as the summer sky. 'The blond guy?'

'No, that's George. He's cute too, but Idris's parents are LOADED!' Belle winks. '*Much* better boyfriend material. Omigosh, look!' She points at a girl with short spiky red hair studying the canteen noticeboard, nodding along to her earphones and munching on a carrot stick. 'Freaky Freya is singing to herself again! Lame!'

'So lame!' I agree, but the mean words taste sour in my mouth. I've got nothing against Freya. She's got an amazing singing voice, and I think her hair's really cool . . . but only an idiot would contradict their one and only friend. I am all too aware how little it would take for *me* to be in Freya's shoes. Just a few more bad decisions (like the salad) and Belle could easily realize that *I'm* lame too, then *I'd* be the loner in the dining room, like I was that first day.

Besides, I reason, Freya seems happy enough by herself, jigging away to her music – and it's not like she can hear us with her earphones in, so no harm done, right?

'What's she doing now?' Belle frowns, moving closer as Freya writes something on a notice. 'Omigosh, she's auditioning for the school *musical*? It's *Wicked*! Anni, we should totally audition!'

My stomach clenches.

'Can't you just see me as Glinda?' Belle bats her eyelashes.

'Absolutely. You should *totally* audition – you'd be amazing!' I gush. 'But I really, *really* can't.' I get tongue-tied at the best of times and cannot think of a single thing worse than standing on a stage in front of a roomful of strangers, trying to sing!

'Come on, Anni!' Belle nudges me, and I nearly drop my tray. 'You can't be any worse than Freaky Freya!'

I freeze. I can't believe she said that, with Freya standing right in front of us! But Freya doesn't even turn. Her music must be really loud. *Phew*.

'Besides, I need my BFF for moral support!'

I bite my lip, totally torn. Just minutes ago, Belle was telling me to make my own decisions, and this one's a no-brainer . . . but maybe being a good friend is more important?

'*Please*, Anni,' she wheedles. 'Don't let me down – I can't do it without you.'

Decision made.

'OK.'

'*Yes!*' Belle cries, scribbling our names on the list. 'You're a star, Anni Sanchez. We're going to rock this audition!'

A warm feeling rushes through me and I smile. But as I follow Belle into the crowded audition room half an hour later, that warmth has turned into stone-cold fear. Somehow I'd thought it'd only be Year 8s auditioning – which would be bad enough – but the room is full of kids from *all* year groups. There's Freya, and Idris, and – omigosh – George! I look away quickly as he glances over, feeling sick with nerves. I am *so* out of my depth.

'Belle,' I hiss. 'I can't do this!'

'Don't be silly!' She laughs. 'It'll be fun. Besides, what else are we going to do all lunchtime? It's thundering outside.'

I glance at the pouring rain, but even standing out there getting drenched seems like a better option.

Suddenly Ms Davis, our drama teacher, claps her hands. 'Right, everyone, let's get warmed up!'

My cheeks are already about as warm as they can possibly get, but I copy her as she leads us through the stretches.

'Now, I'm going to play some music, and I want you all to move around the room pretending to be animals.'

What? It's one thing copying a few dance moves, singing, or reading from a script, but pretending to be an *animal*? In front of everyone? I did not sign up for *that*. What if I make a complete fool of myself? But I can't just stand here doing nothing either! My heart patters in my chest as I gaze around, panicking. Freya is snuffling around the hall like a pig, and soon I recognize rabbits, cats, dogs, and a bunch of guys leaping around like monkeys. Everyone's joining in – except me. *Pick an animal, Anni, quick!* But what? Belle swoops past, fluttering her fingers daintily like a bird, and I do the same – maybe we could be a flock? – but she rolls her eyes, and her voice rings in my ears: 'You're such a sheep, Anni!' So I sit down in the corner, trying to make myself as small and invisible as possible. I'm not going to get into the musical anyway, and if anyone asks, I'll just say I'm a sheep. Fitting, huh?

'Great job, guys!' Ms Davis claps her hands as the music stops. 'Now we're going to learn some choreography.'

I join the back line, just behind Belle, so no one will see me. Ms Davis steps to the left, spins once, twice, then kicks her legs, and we all copy her. So far, so good. But soon the steps start to get more complicated. I just about manage to keep up, but then I notice Belle starting to fall behind. Her frown deepens as she's late with a sidestep, kicks with the wrong leg, then when it comes to the final big spin, she twirls once, loses her balance – and falls over!

Everyone gasps. Belle's face turns bright pink, but before I can help her up, she scrambles to her feet and rushes out.

Oh no!

MAX

'Max!' Ben cries, hurrying over to me in the changing rooms after school. 'Ready for the big match?'

'Am I ever!' I reply, pulling on my old football boots. I really hope they don't let me down. We NEED to beat Farlington!

'Did I tell you my dad's coming to watch?' Ben says. 'Only you said your parents can't make it, so—'

'So *what*?' I interrupt irritably. *Is he trying to rub it in?*

'So I was wondering . . .' Ben continues hesitantly. 'Could we ask Mr Hardy if we can switch positions? Only Dad's never seen me score a goal and—'

'No way! Ben, this is the Cup Final – we need to win!'

His face falls and I immediately feel terrible. I didn't mean to imply Ben's rubbish.

'What I mean is, you're a great striker, but—'

'Ready, boys?' Mr Hardy cries, bounding into the changing rooms. 'We need to put our best foot forward today – goals, goals, goals. Got it, Sanchez? I'm counting on you!'

'Got it!' I grin.

'Excellent!' He beams. 'Bridgehill School – go, go, go!'

We all cheer and I catch up with Ben as we run out on to the pitch.

'Listen, I'm sorry, mate,' I say. 'Maybe next time, OK?'

'Whatever.' He shrugs, walking away to his midfield position.

My heart sinks. But it's not my fault his dad's never seen him score – he hardly ever comes to watch. Ben can't expect everything to change the one time his dad bothers to turn up. Especially when the *Cup* is at stake!

And revenge, I think, spotting Jake. After all, it's Jake's fault I smashed the window, *and* his fault I had to spend all lunchtime in stupid detention. On my birthday.

'Hey, Sanchez!' he calls. 'Are you having a *smashing* day? Get it? Hope the school's boarded up all its windows!'

'Keep dodging balls, Kane – you're good at that,' I counter, but he just laughs. I'm going wipe that smug smile off his face if it's the last thing I do.

Suddenly the whistle blows.

Almost immediately, Harry, our central midfielder, intercepts a Farlington pass and is off like a shot. What a start!

'To me, Harry – to me!' I cry, racing forward. But before he can pass, a Farlington defender tackles him, wins the ball and lobs it to the other end of the pitch. *No!* They pass it between themselves for ages, forcing our defenders to run around madly, trying to mark them, while our goalie, Jamie, watches nervously, waiting for the inevitable. Suddenly their striker surges forward as if to shoot, but at the last minute lays it off to an oncoming midfielder who drills it towards the bottom-right corner of the net. It's a cunning move, and poor Jamie falls to the floor empty-handed – but luckily the shot goes wide! It's our goal kick!

'Whew, that was close, eh, Ben?' I grin as I jog past him.

'What?' he says distractedly, scanning the crowd. But there's no sign of his dad.

Looks like it's not just my parents who are a let-down.

ANNI

'So what're you gonna wear?' Belle asks as we walk home from school.

I blink. 'Wear?'

'For your party, duh!' She giggles.

'Party?' I blink, surprised. 'I didn't think you'd be in the mood after . . . earlier?' She's been really quiet all afternoon, and if it were me, I'd just want to crawl under my duvet and never come out.

'You mean the silly audition? Oh Anni, sweetie, I'm so over it.' Belle laughs. 'The musical's bound to be totally lame anyway. I mean, did you see the other people auditioning? Like Freaky Freya? Can you imagine having to hang out with them for weeks on end? Nightmare!'

'Totally!' I agree, relieved and filled with admiration.

Belle's so strong. I wish I was more like her.

'Besides, it's your *birthday*, Anni, and I'm your best friend! I'm not going to let anything spoil it. Just give me ten minutes to get changed, then I'll come and help you get ready.' She races off down the road, her red mane bouncing, and I grin. She's such a good friend.

I hurriedly get ready, then when the doorbell rings fifteen minutes later I skip downstairs to answer it. This is so exciting!

'Why aren't you dressed up yet?' Belle cries, horrified. 'People are going to be arriving in ten minutes!'

I glance down at my black jeans and black top. I thought I *was* dressed up. But next to Belle in her amazing red dress, I guess I do look a bit scruffy.

'Um, I couldn't decide what to wear,' I fib.

'Don't worry – I'm on the case!' Belle cries, dashing up to my bedroom and rummaging through my pitiful wardrobe. 'Don't you have any dresses at *all*?' she wails.

I shake my head. 'My friends back in London were mainly tomboys.'

'Ugh, *tomboys*? Anni, you're a *teenage girl* – you need to dress like one! I'd run back and fetch you something of mine, but there's just no time. Do you at least have anything that isn't *black*? Ooh, what's this?' She picks up the pink top I unwrapped this morning. 'Wait, what *is* this? A tent?'

I cringe. 'Mum gave it to me for my birthday.'

'Yikes!' Belle winces. 'But maybe we could do something with it. Put it on.'

I obey.

'Wow, that colour's actually lovely on you – really feminine.' Belle smiles. 'But the shape is just . . . well . . . shapeless!'

I nod miserably.

'I know!' Belle says suddenly, and before I realize what she's doing, she grabs the scissors off my desk and cuts a huge slit up the front.

I gasp. 'Belle!'

'Hang on!' She grins, grabbing the two ends and tying them in a knot. 'There! That's better!'

'But . . . my stomach's bare!' I protest, hugging my midriff.

'Duh! That's the whole point!' She laughs. 'Anni, you've got a great figure, you should show it off.'

I feel my cheeks grow warm, despite my bare skin. Belle thinks I've got a great figure? Really? But what would Mum think about my outfit – especially about cutting up her gift? I turn to look in the mirror, but Belle quickly covers it with my dressing gown.

'No mirrors till I've finished. You look lovely, trust me.'

'But—'

'You do trust me, don't you, Anni?'

She stares into my eyes – it feels like a test.

'Yes, of course . . .'

'Great!' She beams, leading me over to my bed. 'Makeover time! My mum always says "a girl should never be without her war-paint".' She pulls out her make-up bag and cranks up the stereo.

I bite my lip, still worried about my top. But I haven't got anything else to wear, and it's not like I can exactly *un*-cut it. Besides, I can always get changed before Mum comes home . . .

'Close your eyes!' Belle smiles, brandishing a tiny sponge, and I obey, trying to keep still as she sweeps it over my face. It feels funny – but nice. I've never really worn make-up before (mainly because I don't even have any – Dad says I'm too young), but as Belle transforms me I've never felt so special. I feel like I'm in one of those movie montages where the ugly duckling becomes a swan.

'Stop smiling!' Belle orders as she applies my eyeshadow. 'Your eyes are all creased.'

'Sorry!' I laugh, but I can't help it. 'Can I look yet?'

'Nope, not till I'm finished. I've got some sparkly pink nail varnish that matches your top perfectly! Here.' She tosses me the tiny bottle. 'Now you just need some earrings to finish the look. Have you got any danglies?'

'No.' I don't have any jewellery, but I can't possibly admit that to Belle.

'But your mum does – she had an amazing pair of gold ones on last weekend. You could borrow those?'

'I can't,' I say, frowning as I carefully paint my nails. 'They're for pierced ears.'

'Oh, that's right.' Suddenly Belle's eyes light up. 'Could *I* borrow them? I forgot to bring mine.'

Borrow Mum's earrings? From her room? Without asking? 'Er, I'm not sure.'

'Come on, she won't mind me borrowing one itty-bitty pair of earrings just for a few hours, will she?'

'Um . . .'

'And I *have* lent you all my make-up – well, *given* it, really, as I'll never get it back.'

'But they're not mine,' I reason. 'If they were, of course I'd lend them to you.'

'Exactly! And your mum's just as cool as you, right?'

I bite my lip.

'Besides,' Belle continues, 'what time did you say she's due home?'

'Six thirty, I think.'

'Perfect! I'll have them back in her room way before then – she'll never even know!' She jumps up.

'Wait!' I cry, and Belle freezes, her green eyes suddenly cold as she frowns at me. Uh-oh. I don't want to upset her, especially after she's been so kind, doing my makeover and throwing me a party. And if the earrings are replaced before Mum's even home, what's the harm? 'I'll get them for you.'

'Don't be silly, you've got wet nails – I'll be back in a sec!' Belle grins, disappearing out the door, leaving me with an uneasy feeling in the pit of my stomach.

But it's just one pair of earrings – what's the worst that could happen?

MAX

When the half-time whistle blows, it's still nil–nil.

'Come on, team!' Mr Hardy cries, passing slices of orange round the changing room. 'Pull your socks up!'

'It's not my *socks* that are the problem; it's these stupid *boots*!' I grumble. They're old, and the studs are so worn down they don't grip properly, especially on the wet grass. If only I'd got my new boots . . .

'No excuses!' Mr Hardy barks. 'Work as a team – we can do this!'

Everyone nods, but I'm not feeling confident any more, and only Ben is smiling as we head back outside. As I follow his gaze I realize why. His dad's finally made it.

Lucky him, I think with a pang of envy, followed by guilt. Maybe we *should've* switched positions. It's not like I've scored yet.

'What's the matter, Maxie?' Jake calls, swinging in their goalmouth like a monkey. 'Tasting the bitterness of defeat already?'

'As if!' I snap, my stomach hardening.

Straight from the kick-off, I pass the ball to Harry, but no – Farlington intercept! They retain possession for most of the half, passing it from player to player. Finally, after what feels like hours, they take a shot – on target! Fortunately, Jamie catches the ball easily and kicks it straight down to our end. I sprint after it, but a defender gets there first. That becomes the pattern for the rest of the game: me desperately chasing after every ball, determined to win it and score a goal. It's exhausting, it's a terrible strategy – I'm playing for myself, not as part of a team – and I can hear Mr Hardy yelling at me from the sidelines, but I don't care. There's a fire in my belly and I will stop at nothing – *nothing* – to get the ball.

Finally one of their team fluffs a pass – and I seize the ball! Adrenaline speeds through my veins as I sprint down the pitch, weaving between defenders towards Jake, towards the goal that will win the match for us and wipe that smug smile off his stupid face forever. As I draw nearer he begins to look nervous, and I grin. This is it! I'm just feet away from victory, from revenge . . .

But I didn't factor in Kyle, Farlington's giant of a centre-back. He looms out of nowhere, and no matter how hard I try to dodge him – one way, then another – he blocks me at every turn.

'Max!' Ben yells. 'Over here!'

I look up. He's on the far side of the pitch, running towards the goal, unmarked, but I hesitate. Ben's not our best goal-scorer. *I* am. This is my moment and there can only be seconds left.

Besides, this is personal. I try again to swerve round Kyle – and he trips me up! I sprawl to the ground, clutching my shin in agony.

'Oh no, Sanchez!' Jake laughs. 'Not another ickle bruise?'

I glare at him but his smile disappears as the ref blows his whistle and I realize where I'm lying.

We've got a penalty!

ANNI

My bedroom door flies open so suddenly, I almost drop the bottle of nail varnish.

'Ta-da!' Belle cries, striking a pose. 'What do you think?'

I gasp. She's not only wearing Mum's dangly gold earrings, but her favourite high heels too!

'Cool, huh?' Belle grins. 'I found them by the wardrobe – don't they make my legs look longer?'

'Belle!' I cry. 'You can't wear those!'

'Why not? They fit perfectly and your mum will never know.'

'But—'

Suddenly the doorbell rings.

'That'll be the first guests!' Belle squeals.

Panic flutters in my stomach. Someone came? This is actually happening?

'Don't worry, birthday girl, I'll let them in. You stay here, let your nails dry, then come and make a big dramatic entrance!' She winks at me. 'Now, no peeking, remember. In fact . . .' She grabs my mirror and totters out.

'Belle!' I protest.

'See you in a bit!' she calls, click-clacking downstairs. I hear her open the door and talk to someone, but I can't tell who. Suddenly music blasts on and the floor beneath me starts shaking, the *thud-thud-thud* drowning out everything else.

I blow on my nails until *finally* they're dry, then I rush out on to the landing and listen. Above the music I can hear people chatting and laughing downstairs. People *came* – to *my* party! – and they're having a *good time*! I feel dizzy with relief, followed by a rush of gratitude to Belle. None of this would've been possible without her – she's such a good friend! Now I just have to go downstairs and face everyone. Easy, right? But my legs tremble as I force one foot in front of the other. I really wish Belle was with me. Everything seems so much easier with her beside me. My heart hammers as I reach the lounge door and I take a deep breath, bracing myself for my big entrance.

This is my house.

This is my party.

I can do this.

I *can*.

On three.

One . . . two . . .

Suddenly the door flies open and a girl I don't know pushes past me, knocking me backwards. Then my jaw drops. Omigosh! That is not a *few* people! Crowds of kids fill the room, sprawling on the sofa, perching on the sideboard, surfing through the TV channels, and dancing in every available space as the music thuds relentlessly on. Most of them I'm not sure I've ever *seen* before, let alone know . . .

'Hi!' I cry, but no one even looks up. '*Hello!*'

Still nothing.

So much for making a big entrance!

I scan the faces quickly, but there's no sign of Belle.

'Belle?' I call anxiously, struggling through the noisy throng to the kitchen, but she's not there either, though another dozen kids are. Most of them seem much older than me, and are sitting on the kitchen counters tucking into the contents of our fridge! There are discarded wrappers all over the floor, and they've only been here ten minutes! My heart stops as I notice a pool of something that looks like blood . . . but then I spot a carton beside it. Tomato juice! *Thank goodness!* I quickly clean it up, and try to put the juice back in the fridge – but there's a blonde girl leaning against it.

'Excuse me!' I shout, but I can barely hear myself over the thumping music. I tap her on the shoulder.

She turns, then frowns. 'Who're you?'

'I'm Anni!' I smile, but her frown deepens.

'Who?'

My smile slips. 'Anni. This is my party?'

'Oh, right.' She gives me a thumbs-up. 'Cool party!'

'Thanks.' I beam. 'What's your name?' But she's already turned to talk to someone else.

I hesitate, then tap her shoulder again. She looks round, annoyed.

'Hi, me again. Sorry. Could I just . . .' I reach for the fridge door, and she huffs, but moves aside. 'Have you seen Belle?' I ask anxiously as I put the carton away.

'Who's Belle?'

This time my smile freezes on my face. If she doesn't know Belle, then how did she get *invited*?

'Um, she's got red curly hair and she's wearing a red dress?'

'Oh, the girl with too much make-up? She was in here about ten minutes ago, but I dunno where she went. Sorry!'

My cheeks burn. *Do I have too much make-up on as well?* I flip my hair over my face as I push my way through the house. 'Belle!' I yell desperately. There are people everywhere – in the hall, sitting on the stairs. Then the front door opens and yet *more* strangers barge inside – but no Belle. Why isn't she controlling who comes in? *Where is she?!*

'Belle!' I struggle back into the lounge where a group of guys are jumping on the sofa yelling at the TV!

'No! Stop! Excuse me!' I tug the nearest guy's arm. 'Would you mind, um, getting down?'

'What? Can't hear you!'

'Shh!' another guys scolds, elbowing him. 'Can't hear the match!'

'Oi! Don't push me!' the first guy cries, grabbing a cushion and whacking him round the head with it.

'Pillow fight!' someone yells, and immediately the whole lounge turns into a battleground – girls squealing, guys yelling, cushions flying – and all I can do is stare, open-mouthed, frozen in panic.

Where's Belle?!

MAX

'Max!' Ben calls, running over. 'Are you OK?'

'Poor Maxie, did you hurt your leggy-weggy?' Jake coos and I scowl at him.

'I can manage!' I snap, shaking Ben off as he tries to help me up. Gingerly I test my weight on my injured leg, then wince. It really kills.

'Maybe you should rest it for a bit?' Ben frowns.

'So you can take my place, and take my penalty, huh, Ben?' I retort, my chest tight. 'Just like you wanted?'

'What?' He blinks. 'No, that's not what I meant! But you can't take the penalty if you're injured!'

'Watch me!' Limping, I pick up the ball, and place it on the spot. Now it's just me and Jake. I meet his gaze and he narrows his eyes, poised on tiptoes, arms outstretched.

But the odds are in my favour. Penalties are SO much easier to score than to save. After all, the goalmouth is huge – Jake can't defend it all. As long as I strike it hard enough into a corner, he doesn't stand a chance.

I take a deep breath, flex my fingers, then run. I kick the ball as hard as I can, a spasm of pain shooting up my injured leg, but I don't care. It'll all be worth it if we win.

As if in slow motion, the ball sails perfectly towards the top-right corner . . . straight into Jake's waiting hands.

'NOOO!' I wail, slumping to my knees.

'Thanks, Maxie!' Jake yells, spinning the ball on his finger, showing off. Then he drop-kicks it all the way to the other end of the pitch. I can barely watch as their striker kicks it straight past a dazed Jamie, deep into the back of our net – just as the final whistle blows.

I can't believe it.

They've won.

Jake won.

And it's all my fault.

ANNI

I stare helplessly around the war zone that used to be my lounge. *How can this possibly get worse?!*

Suddenly there's a smashing sound from the hallway, and Nana's crystal-cut vase shatters into a million pieces on the floor.

NO!

Dad is going to kill me! I think it's an antique. Well, *was* . . .

This whole party is a complete and utter *disaster*!

I hurry over, carefully scoop up the remains, drop them in the bin beneath the hall mirror, then freeze.

Omigosh – is that *me*?! I gawp at my reflection. My hair is humungous, my lips bright pink to match my top, and my eyes are ringed in green, blue and purple eyeliner and surrounded in dark shadow. I look like I've been punched – twice! Is this *fashion*?

'Anni!' Belle cries, rushing towards me. 'There you are!'

'Belle! I've been looking for you everywhere!'

'Well, obvs not *everywhere*!' She laughs.

Suddenly someone screams and we hurry into the lounge to find the dancing girls pulling handfuls of feathers out of the burst cushions and throwing them at each other, while the guys are now full-on wrestling on the rug, knocking drinks flying.

Belle gasps. 'Anni, this party is out of CONTROL!'

'I know!' I wail miserably.

'It's better than I ever hoped!' She beams, eyes gleaming. 'No one is *ever* going to forget this. It'll be talked about for *weeks*!'

I stare at her. She seriously thinks that's a *good* thing?

'Omigosh – Idris came!' Belle squeals, shimmying towards him.

'Watch out, everyone!' Idris cries. 'It's Bombshell Belle!'

'What're you talking about?' another guy yells. 'I thought her nickname was Dumb-Belle?'

My eyebrows shoot up. *What?*

'She's got a new one now – didn't you hear?' Idris shouts over the music. 'She totally fell on her arse at the audition today!'

As everyone bursts out laughing, Belle freezes. Her

face flushes beetroot-pink, then she turns to run, but stumbles in Mum's high heels and topples dramatically to the floor.

'Not again!' The boys laugh even harder. Poor Belle!

'Are you OK?' I cry, rushing over.

'No! Ow! I think I've broken my leg!'

'Oh NO!' *What should I do?* I grab the phone and dial 999 in a panic.

'*Stupid shoes!*' Belle scowls, pulling one off, and I gasp. The heel of Mum's sandal has completely snapped off! She's going to *kill* me!

MAX

If looks could kill, I'd have died at least fifty times. Mr Hardy hates me, Ben hates me, the entire football team hates me – make that the entire school! My shin's still throbbing, and Jake was just so utterly smug I wanted to punch him in his stupid face. In fact I probably would have, if Mr Hardy hadn't dragged me into the changing rooms to yell at me for ten minutes for not being a 'team player' and announce he's going to 'have to seriously consider my place on the team'. I'm actually glad Mum and Dad *couldn't* come. As I hobble miserably home, I just want to forget all about it.

And suddenly I do, as an ambulance speeds past – and stops outside my house!

Despite my injured shin, I race home, my heart pounding.

Kids I don't even recognize are racing out the door and – oh my gosh – has there been an EARTHQUAKE? The lounge is a total bombsite, filled with people, cushions, feathers – and paramedics! They're bending over someone lying on the floor – *please not Anni*! I rush over, fear pulsing through me, but it's her friend Belle, looking so cross she can't be badly hurt.

'Max! Anni! Are you OK?' Mum and Dad race in behind me, then stop dead, eyes bulging as they stare round the lounge, mouths gaping like electrified goldfish.

Then Dad's gaze lands on me and his expression changes from fear to shock to anger in nanoseconds.

'Party's over!' he yells, and everyone rushes for the door. 'What the heck were you *thinking*, Max?'

'*What?* It wasn't me – I just walked in!' I protest. That is SO typical. Why am I always the one they blame for everything?

Mum hurries over to the paramedics tending to Belle. 'Sweetheart, are you OK?'

'Yes, just a twisted ankle, nothing serious,' says a paramedic. 'But she mustn't walk on it.'

'I'll drive her home,' Dad says.

'No! I'm fine! Really!' Belle insists, trying to stand. 'I can walk . . . *Ow!*'

'Sit down, sweetheart,' Mum says, helping her to a chair. 'Thank you for your help,' she tells the paramedics as they leave. 'What happened?'

'Stupid shoes broke.' Belle scowls.

'Are they . . . are they *my* shoes?' Mum gasps, staring at the broken sandal.

'Anni said you wouldn't mind me borrowing them,' Belle says quickly.

'*Anni* did?'

Belle nods. 'She said you wouldn't be back till six thirty either.'

Dad's face hardens. 'Our neighbour phoned. She said it was an emergency.'

Nosy Nora strikes again. Typical. If there was a contest for Nosiest Next-Door Neighbour in the North-East, she'd win hands down.

Mum frowns. 'Where *is* Anni?'

Belle points to the corner of the room, and my jaw drops as I spot Anni cowering behind the bookcase. I can't believe that's actually my sister! Her stomach's bare, her top's torn, and she looks like she had a fight with a box of face paint – and lost!

'Anni?' Dad gasps. 'I didn't even *recognize* you!'

'Is that . . . your new top?' Mum asks quietly.

Anni nods miserably, hugging her bare midriff.

'Go and get changed at once,' Dad barks. 'Wipe that muck off your face, then you can clean up down here. I am SO disappointed in you.'

'I'm sorry.' Anni hangs her head and slumps miserably towards the staircase.

'What were you *thinking*?' Mum demands. 'You've never done anything like this before – it's just not like you!'

'You're right, it's not.' Dad rounds on Belle. 'This was *your* idea, wasn't it, young lady?'

'What? No! As if!' Belle protests. 'Anni, tell them.'

Anni freezes on the stairs, her gaze flicking between Belle and our parents, torn.

'Tell them it was your idea, Anni!' Belle insists.

'It was . . . it was my idea,' Anni repeats unconvincingly. She's always been a terrible liar.

'Now you're *lying* for her?' Dad says angrily. 'That's it. You're a bad influence, Belle. You're banned from being friends with Anni any more.'

'What?!' Anni's eyes widen in horror. 'But . . . Belle's my best friend!'

Make that *only* friend.

'Case closed,' Dad snaps. 'Come on, Belle, I'll take you home.'

'No, please!' Tears fill Anni's eyes as she rushes down the stairs. 'Please, Dad, don't do this.'

'You're better off without her.'

'And *I'm* better off without *you*, Anni! Thanks for sticking up for me – *not*!' Belle snaps as Dad helps her outside. 'I try to do something nice for you, and you get me in trouble? Thanks a lot! My mum's gonna kill me – and I bet you'll blame me for the broken vase, too!'

43

'What vase?' Dad asks, just as Belle slams the front door behind them.

'Tell me she doesn't mean Nana's vase,' Mum says sharply.

Anni winces.

'Oh, *Anni*!'

'I'm sorry, I'm so sorry, about everything. I never meant for any of this to happen!' Anni sobs. 'I'll do anything you want to make up for it. You can ground me for a year, you can stop my pocket money, but please, Mum, don't stop me being friends with Belle!'

Mum sighs. 'You'll make new friends, sweetheart.'

'Like it's that easy!' Anni's face crumples as she rushes upstairs.

Poor Anni. I think that's the worst punishment she could ever get.

'You too, Max.' Mum folds her arms. 'Upstairs. Birthday or no birthday, you're both grounded for a month.'

'*What?*' I protest. 'But I didn't do anything! I just walked in – honest!'

'The school rang,' she says coldly. 'We know about the broken window.'

Uh-oh.

'Which you're going to pay for, by the way.'

Great. There goes my pocket money for the next five years.

'Or Mrs MacCready says you can do chores for her instead.'

'No way!' Hours of slave labour with that awful woman? That's worse than being broke!

'*And* the school told us you failed your maths test.' Mum glares at me, eyes blazing. 'So you're going to be doing extra studying for the rest of the term – instead of football.'

'*What?*'

'You heard me. Now go to your room.'

'But what about our birthday tea – and presents?'

'When you can act like you're thirteen, you can have them,' Mum snaps. 'Upstairs – *now!*'

I can't believe it. *No birthday presents, no birthday tea, and no football?* This is the worst birthday ever!

ANNI

This is the worst birthday in the history of forever.

I stare at my bedside clock watching the minutes click slowly, endlessly, past. 23.31. 23.32. I heard Mum and Dad go to bed ages ago, but I can't sleep. The events of the day keep whirling round and round my head, keeping me awake. All the mistakes I made, everything I should've done differently.

But it's too late.

I sigh heavily and trudge downstairs to get a glass of water, but to my surprise I find Max peering into the fridge.

'Max?' I whisper.

'Jeepers, Anni!' He jumps, startled. 'You scared me – even *without* all the face paint!'

I frown. 'What are you doing up?'

'Couldn't sleep. I'm starving.'

'You're *always* starving.'

He nods glumly. 'Especially when I'm miserable.'

I sigh heavily. 'Some birthday, huh?'

'The worst,' he agrees. 'I can't even find anything I feel like eating – not that there's much left after your party.'

'Sorry.' I reach into a cupboard for a glass, then spot a white box hidden at the back. 'What's this?' I frown, pulling it out.

'One way to find out.' Max shrugs, opening it.

My heart plummets. It's our birthday cake.

We both stare at the swirly white icing letters: *Happy Birthday Max and Anni.*

'*Happy Birthday?*' Max scoffs gloomily. 'Yeah, right.'

'Tell me about it.' I sigh. 'I wish we could just wake up and start all over again.'

'Me too.' Max sighs. 'Wait, Anni. That's it! We still get a birthday wish, right?'

I frown. 'What do you mean?'

'Even if we're not allowed to eat any cake, we should still get to make a wish – it's still our birthday, after all.'

'Yeah, for another fifteen minutes,' I say, glancing at the kitchen clock.

'Quick, help me find the candles.'

I raise an eyebrow. 'Seriously?'

'Hurry!'

'OK!' I scrabble through the kitchen drawers, a flicker of excitement fluttering through me, despite the terrible day. I rummage through napkins, corkscrews, chopsticks – but there are no candles.

'It's 11.52! We're running out of time!' Max wails. 'There must be some candles *somewhere*.'

I smile. Once Max has an idea in his head, it's difficult to get it out again. If only he was as dedicated to his schoolwork! I look in the cupboard under the sink – nothing – then try the cupboard under the stairs . . . and find a big bag of presents, all wrapped up and shiny. My heart leaps with excitement, then nosedives as I remember why we haven't opened them.

'Hurry up,' Max hisses. 'We've only got four minutes before midnight!'

'OK,' I glance sadly back at the bag of presents, and there on top is a red-and-white-striped candle! 'Got one!'

'Just one?' Max hisses. 'Oh well, it'll have to do. Come on, let's get this sucker lit, and fast!'

I stab the stripy candle into the cake, and it makes a strange hissing noise as Max lights it.

'Huzzah!' he cries. Where *does* he pick up these phrases? 'Right, let's both wish to start our birthday over again. Agreed?' His eyes glint in the candlelight.

I nod.

'One . . . two . . . three . . .'

We both take a deep breath and blow. I know it's silly, that birthday wishes don't come true, but I still feel a tingle as the flame flickers out – and then suddenly relights itself!

'It's one of those prank relighting candles!' Max moans. 'Typical Dad!'

'But we have to blow it out,' I insist. 'It's a fire hazard!'

Max rolls his eyes. 'Don't forget to wish again! Go!'

We keep blowing and wishing until finally the flame disappears for good, leaving a wisp of smoke snaking lazily into the air.

'Phew!' Max sighs as the clock chimes midnight. 'Just in time.'

'Thank goodness.' I giggle. 'I'm exhausted!'

Max grins at me and I smile.

Whether it comes true or not, this has been the best moment of this terrible day.

And it's finally over.

DAY 2

MAX

The shriek of the smoke alarm wakes me with a jerk. *Not again!*

Footsteps pound down the stairs, followed by a sudden shriek.

'Max!' Mum yells. 'What have I told you about leaving your football kit in the middle of the floor?'

Eh? 'But I didn't!' I protest, hurrying on to the landing. I was still wearing my kit when I got home last night – I only took it off when I went to bed.

'So it just miraculously appeared in the middle of the floor by itself, did it?' Anni scowls, holding up my bag.

'I didn't put it there, honest!' I insist. 'Why do I always get the blame for *everything*?'

'Because it's always your fault!' Anni retorts.

'Twins, please!' Mum cries as she finally manages to silence the smoke alarm. 'Not today. It's your birthday!'

I stare at her.

It's our *what?*

ANNI

Goosebumps prickle down my arms as Mum leads us

into the kitchen. *I must've misheard her.*

'Happy birthday!' Dad cries, presenting us with two plates. 'You like your bacon crispy, right?'

My jaw drops. There was no mishearing that time! My stomach turns as I stare at the burned bacon, and not just because it looks so unappetizing. *What is going on?*

'I . . . I'm not hungry,' Max says, his face turning pale.

'Don't be ridiculous, Max. You're always hungry!' Dad grins. 'Present time! One each before I go to work!'

What? I glance at Max, who looks just as confused as I am.

Dad disappears into the hallway and returns with two brightly wrapped parcels that look identical to the ones we opened yesterday. Sure enough, as I unwrap the paper my cheeks burn with shame.

It's the same pink top.

Miserably, I feel for the tear. But it isn't there. Mum must've sewn it up. Which makes me feel even worse.

'*What?*' Max cries, pulling out the same boots he got yesterday.

Mum nudges Dad. 'I think he likes them!'

'I hope so – they cost enough!' Dad chortles. 'Happy birthday, Max.'

Max stares at the boots, speechless for possibly the first time in his life. Then suddenly he grins, and I'm more confused than ever.

'Thank you! I'm going to go and try them on with my kit right now – why don't you try your new top on too, Anni?'

I blink. 'What?'

'Come on.' He grabs my arm and drags me into the hallway.

'What was that all about?' I hiss as soon as we're out of earshot.

'Anni, don't you get it?' he says excitedly. 'It's our wish – it's come true! It's our birthday all over again!'

'What?' I stare at him. 'Max, don't be ridiculous. That's impossible.'

'No, it's *magic*!'

'Seriously? Max, you're thirteen, not three. There's no such thing as magic.'

'Well what other explanation is there, Miss Smarty-Pants?' he demands, folding his arms. 'Why else would Mum and Dad wish us happy birthday *again* and give us *exactly the same presents*?'

'Well . . .' I rack my brains for a logical reason. It *is* weird. Especially after Max threw such a tantrum over his boots yesterday, and I ruined my top . . .

'And it's a bit of a coincidence that we wished for this *exact* thing to happen last night!' Max adds.

Of course! 'That's *it*!'

'Exactly!' Max grins. 'Our wish came true!'

'No, idiot! Mum and Dad must've *overheard* our wish, and are giving us a chance to redo our birthday!'

'Huh?'

Honestly, sometimes I think I got ALL the brain cells. 'They're giving us an opportunity to show we've learned our lesson, and won't be ungrateful jerks, or throw wild parties this time,' I explain. 'They even said we could have our presents when we start acting like we're thirteen, remember? If we behave better today, maybe we won't even be grounded any more – or banned from playing football.'

'You really think so?' Max says hopefully.

I shrug. 'They did give you football boots, after all!'

Suddenly Dad bustles out of the kitchen. 'Have a great day, you two. I'm really sorry, but I have to work late – again – and so does Mum, but do you both want to invite some friends over for tea?'

'Even Belle?' I cross my fingers.

Dad shrugs. 'Whoever you like.' He ruffles Max's hair as he hurries out the door. 'Score lots of goals, Max!'

'Goals?' Max punches the air. '*Yes!*'

MAX

I can't believe Mum and Dad have un-grounded us *and* I can play football again! It may not be magic, but it's pretty close. We finally got to open our birthday cards too – and Granny's came with a musical badge and *twenty quid*. Result!

'Hey, Max, wait up!' Ben calls, running over and leaping on to my shoulders as I cross the village green.

'Hey, Ben,' I cry happily, surprised that he's even still talking to me, let alone waiting for me. I thought he'd still be really mad after yesterday's match, but that's one of the things I like about Ben – he doesn't hold a grudge. 'Y'all right?'

'Me? I'm fine!' Ben grins. 'How are *you*?'

'Hungry!' I say.

'You're always hungry!' Ben laughs. 'But today's your lucky day, because—'

'Heads up!'

I look up just as a football smacks into the side of my head, knocking me to the ground. 'OUCH!'

Not again?

'Sorry, mate!' a familiar voice calls, and sure enough, there's Jake Kane jogging over.

'Think you're funny, do you?' I yell angrily, scrambling to my feet. 'Stupid smug idiot!'

'Whoa, Maxie. Don't get your knickers in a twist!' Jake cries. 'It was an accident.'

Two mornings in a row? 'Yeah, right!'

'Hope I haven't bruised that pretty ickle face of yours?' He grins. 'You're a delicate lot at Bridgehill, aren't you?'

'Original,' I scoff. 'Can't you come up with a better line today?'

'Whatever.' Jake rolls his eyes. 'Chuck my ball back, mate.'

'Yeah, right, so you can dodge it and make me break another of Mrs MacCready's windows? I don't think so.'

Jake frowns. 'Mrs who?'

'You broke a window?' Ben gasps, eyes wide. 'When? Where?'

'What?' I frown. 'Yesterday. Right there!'

Ben and Jake look where I point. But amazingly the window's now intact. She must have had it fixed already. Great. Emergency window repairs are bound to cost even more.

'Er, think you need to get your eyes tested, mate.' Jake laughs. 'And you're gonna need better reflexes than that to beat us in the match later.'

I freeze. 'What did you say?'

'Max, chill out!' Ben says, pulling me away.

'What's he talking about? What match?'

Ben raises an eyebrow. 'Er, how hard did that football hit you? The Cup Final, of course!'

'What?' My heart lifts. 'Are we having a rematch?'

'Er, we need a *first* match first!' Ben laughs. 'Are you feeling OK? You are looking a bit pale. Here, chocolate always makes me feel better.' He passes me a plastic bag and I pull out another king-size chocolate bar. 'Sorry, didn't have time to wrap it.'

'Huh?'

'Happy birthday anyway!'

My head snaps up. '*What?*'

'Um . . . happy birthday?' Ben says uncertainly. 'It *is* your birthday, right?'

My heart beats faster as I look back at Mrs MacCready's window. It isn't broken. The Cup match is tonight. There's only one possible explanation.

'Yes! It's my *birthday*!' I cry. I was right – *our wish DID come true!*

'Did you *forget*? Ben gasps. 'Oh my gosh, did that knock on the head give you *amnesia*?'

'No – the opposite!' I laugh. 'Ben you will never *believe* what's happened. I've . . . I've sort of gone back in time!'

'Like Doctor Who?' he says excitedly. 'Did you go in a time machine?'

'Well, no, but Anni and I both had a terrible day yesterday, so last night we wished on our birthday candle that we could do it differently, and when we woke up this morning it was today – again! It's magic!'

'Magic?' Ben frowns. 'Is this one of your pranks, Max?'

'No – honest!'

'Prove it.'

'What?'

'Tell me something that's going to happen today.' He folds his arms.

'OK,' I think fast. 'The Year Eight maths test is really hard.'

Ben snorts. 'Duh!'

'Um . . .' I think harder. 'There's going to be veggie lasagne and chicken salad for lunch!'

'Fine, I'll wait till lunchtime and see.'

'No, wait.' There must be *something* that'll prove I'm not lying. Suddenly I snap my fingers. 'Your dad! You're going to ask me to swap positions in the match today because your dad's coming to watch.'

Ben's jaw drops. 'How did you know?'

'Because I've been here before!' I laugh. 'He arrives just after half-time.'

'My dad actually *comes*?' Ben gasps. 'I mean, he always says he'll do his best to get there, but I try not to get my hopes up . . . so if this is a joke, Max, it's really not funny.'

'It's not! Scout's honour!'

'You're not a Scout.'

'Well, no – but Anni was a Brownie!'

'What's that got to do with anything?'

'You'd believe Anni, right? Even if you don't believe me?'

'Well, yes,' Ben says. 'Anni's a very honest person.'

'Come on then!' I grin, grabbing his arm.

ANNI

I cross my fingers nervously as I wait on Belle's wall. Thank goodness Mum and Dad changed their minds about us being friends, but what if Belle's still mad at

56

me? I wish I could've done things differently yesterday. I should never have lied to Mum and Dad – and I'm such a rubbish liar, I just made everything ten times *worse*! – but I should've stuck up for Belle more. After all, the party was just as much my fault as hers. It was her idea, but I didn't have to go along with it. It was *my* house, *my* birthday, *my* responsibility – there's no way she should've got into trouble just for being a good friend. My only friend. I swallow hard as tears sting my eyes. *I can't lose her, I can't . . .*

'Anni!'

I turn, surprised to see Max dragging Ben down the road towards me. 'Anni, tell Ben what day it is!'

'Happy birthday, Anni!' Ben puffs.

I roll my eyes. 'Very funny. It's Friday.'

'What?' Ben frowns. 'No, I'm sure it's Thursday.'

'It is!' Max insists. 'Anni, our wish came true!'

'Not this again.' I sigh. 'Come on, Max. Mum and Dad were just giving us a second chance to be good this morning, that's all.'

'But it's not just Mum and Dad!' Max protests. 'Five minutes ago, Jake taunted me about the Cup Final *today*, and Mrs MacCready's window isn't broken any more! Anni, *it's still our birthday*. Tell her, Ben.'

'I'm so confused,' Ben whimpers, looking genuinely baffled. But then that is kind of his usual expression.

A door slams behind us and Belle storms down her driveway.

'Belle!' I jump up.

'I'm not in the mood, Anni,' she mutters, marching past me, arms folded.

'Belle! Please!' I hurry after her. 'Wait!'

'Anni, come back!' Max calls, but I ignore him.

'Belle, please – I'm really sorry about yesterday. I had no idea Mum and Dad would come home early, or freak out or anything. And I'm so sorry that I didn't—'

'Anni,' Belle snaps, stopping me short, 'I can't understand a word you're saying – especially with your hair all over your face. Can't you at least put it up or something?'

My hands fly to my hair as my cheeks burn. Yesterday she said she liked it loose . . . 'I – I don't have a hairband.'

Belle sighs, pulls a hairband off her wrist and passes it to me. 'Here. It's your first day of being a teenager, after all. You need to look the part.'

I stop dead. 'What?'

'Happy birthday, by the way!' As she strides away I suddenly realize that there's nothing wrong with her ankle . . .

'See!' Max crows, coming up behind me. 'Now you *have* to believe me!'

'I believe you,' Ben adds.

Omigosh! My heart beats fast as I desperately try to make sense of what's happening – and fail.

'I'd like an apology please,' Max says smugly.

'Anni?' Belle turns and frowns. 'Are you coming or what?'

'I . . .' I can't move. I can't believe it. Max was *right*?

'She'll catch you up,' Max calls.

'Whatever.' Belle shrugs, marching away.

I want to run after her, but my mind's racing with too many questions.

'How is this *possible*, Max? How can it *still* be our birthday?'

'I don't know!' He laughs. 'But it doesn't really matter – the point is we're here. Yesterday. Today, I mean. Our birthday. Again! The question is: *now* what do we do?'

'What do you mean?' I frown. 'We have to go to school and sit that awful maths test all over again.'

Ben groans.

'No we don't,' Max argues, his eyes twinkling. 'Think about it. Today is a gift – it's literally *the present*! We need to make the most of it.'

I nod. 'You're right.'

'So let's skip school!' he cries. 'All three of us.'

'*What?*' I stare at him. 'Max, we can't!'

'Why not? Come on, we've already taken the maths test *and* all of today's lessons. Sitting through them again would be a total waste of our do-over day.'

'No it wouldn't!' I argue, incredulous. 'That's the *whole entire point* of a do-over day – we get to do things *better*! We can try to get higher marks on the maths test and not get into trouble.'

Max rolls his eyes. 'Seriously?'

'Yes, *seriously*,' I retort.

'Fine!' Max throws his hands up in frustration. 'Do what you want – but Ben and I are going to have a fun day, bunking off.'

'Um . . . actually I can't,' Ben says. 'Sorry, Max.'

'What?' Max rounds on him. 'You said you believed me!'

'I do!' Ben insists. 'And you said my dad's coming to the match.'

'He is!'

'Then there's no way I can bunk off – or they won't let me play!'

Max frowns. I can almost see the tussle between playing football and bunking off school in his mind. 'Well . . . we could both pretend to be ill, then come back after school and say we're feeling better?'

'Yeah, that wouldn't look suspicious *at all*,' I scoff.

'I'm sorry,' Ben says. 'You bunk off if you like, Max, but I can't. Not today.'

'Oh, I get it,' Max says suddenly, scowling. 'If *I* bunk

off, then *you* can take my place on the team as striker, just like you wanted? Nice, Ben. Great mate you are.'

'No, Max – it's not like that!' Ben protests.

'Don't be so mean, Max,' I chide. 'Come on, Ben, or we'll be late.'

'Yeah, you'd better go, Ben,' Max says bitterly. 'Can't be late for your test. Which you fail, by the way.'

Ugh. Sometimes I can hardly believe Max is my twin at all.

MAX

I can't believe Anni's my twin – she's such a goody-two-shoes! She *always* plays by the rules, *always* does as she's told, she's every teacher's – and Mum and Dad's – pet. She's so BORING! Worst of all, she always makes *me* look bad. Sometimes I wonder if she was swapped at birth or something. Or *I* was?

But Ben's hurt expression as he turns away fills me with guilt. Maybe I was a bit harsh, but I was so *sure* he'd bunk off with me – especially on my birthday!

I sigh. Let Ben and Anni go to stupid school if they want. *I'm* gonna have some fun!

I turn on my heel and sprint down the road, the wind in my hair, the sun on my face, blood pumping in my veins. No maths test for me. No boring lessons, no detention. I can do ANYTHING I WANT! I feel like a wild animal – a gazelle –

a cheetah. I leap up to brush my fingers through the overhanging branches as I run, and the scent of pine needles fills my nose. This is going to be the best birthday ever!

Finally I round a corner, and there it is – the sea! Broad, blue and glistening in the sunshine, the air sticky with the salty smell of seaweed. No wonder Mum and Dad wanted to move here. Living near the sea makes me feel like I'm on a never-ending holiday.

I run across the pebbly beach, drop my bag, pull off my shoes and socks and wade into the crashing waves, gasping as the freezing water fizzes round my ankles like frothy lemonade. I grin as I think of everyone else stuck inside taking the stupid maths test on this glorious sunny day. What a waste!

I pick up a stone and skim it as far as I can, and another, and another. Whoa, that one skimmed *four* times! I punch the air and look around, but the beach is empty. Nobody saw. I can't believe I did my best-ever skim when there was no one to see.

What a waste.

ANNI

What a wasted opportunity! I can't believe the maths test was *just* as hard today, even though I'd already seen all the questions! So much for using today to make up for yesterday's mistakes.

'Belle, how did you do question fifteen?' I ask as we join the lunch queue. After all, she should know the answer: she got full marks. 'The one with the triangle with one side-length missing?'

She sighs. 'Oh, Anni, I'd need a pen and paper, and –'

I rifle through my school bag. 'Here you go.'

'Anni, please. It's lunchtime; I need to *relax*,' she snaps. 'Besides, it's too late. The test is over.'

I sigh miserably. She's right. It's too late to stop me being moved down a set.

'Cheer up. I'll come over and help you study if you like?' Belle offers. 'How about after school? Or we could have a sleepover at the weekend?'

'After school would be great.' I smile. 'Mum and Dad said you could stay for tea, too, but it'll be quite late – they're both working till six thirty.'

'*Really?*' Belle's eyes light up. 'Then I know what'll *really* cheer you up. Hey, guys!' she calls over to a group of Year 9s. 'Party at Anni's house after school. Thirty-three, Elm Road – four o'clock. Be there or be square!'

'No. No party!' I cry, my heart beating fast. No way. *Not after last night.*

'Whatever.' One of the girls shrugs, giving me a weird look.

'Why?' Belle frowns.

'Because . . .' I hesitate. I can't exactly explain – she'll

63

never believe me! 'I – I'm not feeling well,' I lie.

'Uh-huh.' Belle folds her arms, unconvinced. 'Just like Max, eh? Hey, maybe it's *twin*-fluenza!'

'What?' I frown.

'I hear your "dad" rang up and everything.' Belle giggles, making quotation marks with her fingers. 'Classic. Why can't you be more like Max, Anni? He knows how to have fun.'

Great. So now Belle thinks I'm no fun.

Today isn't going any better than yesterday at all.

'Now, what's for lunch?' Belle eyes the counter and I smile. Finally I can do something better!

'Lasagne, please,' I say.

'Really?' Belle raises an eyebrow.

I look up, surprised. I thought that was the *right* choice.

She wrinkles her nose. 'All that grease? You've got to be careful now you're a teenager, you know. In fact . . .' She stares at my face. 'Is that a little spot?'

Oh no! I'd forgotten about my spot.

'Sorry – can I have salad instead, please?'

'Atta girl.' Belle grins at me as we pick up our trays.

Suddenly she nudges me and I nearly drop everything. Again.

'Omigosh, look!' Belle hisses, and I sigh, already knowing what I'll see. 'Freaky Freya is singing to herself again. Lame! Wait, what's she doing now?'

'She's auditioning for the school musical, how totally lame!' I say quickly, hoping to stop a repeat of yesterday. To my surprise, Freya turns and glares at me before marching away. *Oh no!* I thought she couldn't hear us with her earphones in!

'It's not lame, it's *Wicked*!' Belle protests. 'My favourite musical! Anni, we should totally audition! Can't you just see me as Glinda?' She bats her eyelashes.

'Well . . .' I can't tell her she'd be no good, but I need to stop her auditioning. 'Yes, *you'd* be amazing. But look at everyone else who's auditioning,' I say hastily, remembering what she'd said yesterday. 'Do you really want to hang out with them for weeks on end?' I feel terrible saying something so unkind – and I really don't mean it – but I'm desperate.

'Er, weeks on end with *Idris*? Yes *please*!' Belle squeals, pointing at his name on the list. 'He's super-cute, and SUPER-LOADED!'

'And super-*mean*,' I add, remembering how he mocked Belle at the party yesterday.

'What are you talking about?'

'Oh, I just heard a rumour . . .' I shrug. After all, the party hasn't technically happened!

'Don't believe rumours, Anni. You should get to know people yourself. And the musical is the perfect way to get to know Idris!' Belle beams, scribbling our names on the list.

'What? No! I can't. I told you, I'm not feeling well,' I protest. After all, Belle said yesterday that she couldn't audition without me.

'Oh, you'll be fine. You're probably just hungry!'

I stare at my shrivelled salad miserably, my appetite totally gone.

MAX

My stomach rumbles loudly. Must be lunchtime!

But then I have an awful thought. *What am I going to eat?* I check my pockets – I always carry an emergency pound – but there's only few coins left after using the phone box to call school pretending to be Dad. If only I hadn't broken my mobile phone last week! If only I hadn't already eaten the chocolate bar Ben gave me! If only I'd brought Granny's twenty-pound note with me! My heart plummets faster than Cristiano Ronaldo faking a foul. I SO did not think this through.

My stomach grumbles again and I shiver as the sun goes behind a cloud.

What should I do?

I could go home . . . but Nosy Nora would be bound to catch me and call Mum and Dad, and they'd ground me for life.

I could go back to school and say I'm feeling better . . . but how lame would *that* be? I've been given this extra day – I don't want to waste it. Besides, Anni would never let me live it down . . .

Suddenly there's a raucous cry overhead and something wet plops on my head.

Yuck! Dive-bombed by a seagull on my birthday! Could things get any worse?

SPLAT!

Not *again!* I scowl at the birds. Are they ganging up on me, or what?

Suddenly a bright flash fills the sky and I realize it's not seagulls after all . . . I forgot about the *thunderstorm!*

ANNI

I trudge after Belle as she skips happily into the dance studio for the audition. It's like watching a car crash happen in slow motion, knowing there's nothing I can do to stop it. Except . . . I could tell her the truth? I bite my lip. She'd probably think I'm completely crazy; she might even laugh at me . . . But I have to take that risk. She's my best friend – I can't let her embarrass herself.

'Belle,' I hiss. 'I need to tell you something really important.'

'Ooh, what?' Her eyes sparkle.

I glance at everyone streaming in around us. 'Not

here. Outside.' I tug at her arm.

'Anni, the audition's about to start. Tell me here, or afterwards – up to you.'

I sigh. Afterwards won't be any good! I lean close and whisper in her ear, quickly explaining about the wish, and what happened in the audition yesterday. When I've finished she stares at me, wide-eyed.

'Wow,' she says eventually, shaking her head. 'I can't believe it.'

'I know – isn't it incredible?!'

'No, I can't believe you'd make up such a ridiculous, *offensive* story just because *you* don't want to audition.'

'What? No!'

'As if *I'd* be the one to embarrass myself!' she scoffs. 'You're just worried about embarrassing *yourself*!'

'No, Belle, honestly, I can prove it! Ms Davis is going to make us act like animals – and Freya is going to pretend to be a pig!'

Belle snorts. 'Fitting.'

I glance anxiously at Freya, who's stretching nearby. *Did she hear?*

'Now I'm going to play some music,' Ms Davis says. 'And I want you all to move around the room pretending to be animals.'

Belle looks up at me, surprise and confusion flickering across her face, and I smile. Any second now Freya will start acting like a pig and Belle will *have* to believe me.

But to my surprise, Freya spreads her arms and starts swooping round the room, hooting like an owl.

Belle scowls at me, then flutters away, leaving me confused and anxious. Why didn't Freya choose the same animal as yesterday? Can other things change? Like maybe Belle won't mess up her dancing this time?

Or did Freya overhear us and *deliberately* choose a different animal? I guess there's only one way to find out . . .

As we copy Ms Davis's dance steps, I cross my fingers tightly, desperately hoping that things will go differently this time. But no – Belle's soon falling behind again. Her face turns pink and my heart beats faster as she's late with a sidestep, kicks with the wrong leg, and – here comes the big spin . . . *I have to do something quick!*

Panicking, I throw myself at Belle and we both topple to the ground.

Everyone gasps.

'Whoops – sorry, Belle!' I giggle. 'I've got two left feet!'

Everyone laughs, except Freya, who gives me a strange look, and Belle, who glares at me, scrambles to her feet, then rushes out.

Oh no!

'Belle, wait!' I cry, hurrying after her to the girls loos.

But as I race inside, her cubicle slams shut. 'Belle, are you OK?'

No answer.

'Belle, I'm so sorry – I'm so clumsy.'

Silence.

'Belle . . .' I hesitate. 'I know you don't believe me, but—'

Suddenly the door to the loos flies open.

'Anni!' Freya cries, rushing in. 'There you are. Quick – it's time for your singing audition.'

'What? No! I can't –'

'Why? Is it too *lame*?' Freya folds her arms and my stomach lurches. She *did* hear me earlier.

'I'm sorry – I didn't really mean that . . .'

Her expression softens. 'Then why not come back and audition? You did really well in the dancing.'

'Yeah, right,' I scoff. 'Apart from the bit where I fell over.'

'Yeah,' Freya lowers her voice. '*Deliberately*. I was watching you. You did all the other steps perfectly – but Belle didn't. And she was losing her balance *before* you fell on her. You're a good friend, Anni, and I can tell that you're a really nice person – deep down.'

Ouch. *Deep down?*

'But don't let Belle make you someone you're not.'

I frown. 'I'm not.' Am I?

'And don't let her ruin your chance to be in the musical,' Freya whispers. 'I think you'd be brilliant.'

'Oh, no, you don't understand,' I say quickly, forgetting to keep my voice low. 'I never *wanted* to be in the musical—'

'Don't we know it!' Belle cries suddenly, storming out of her cubicle and startling Freya. 'But you didn't have to ruin *my* chances.'

'I didn't!' I protest. 'It wasn't your fault I fell over on top of you – it won't count against you!'

'No, but I was already getting steps wrong before then, thanks to you! I can't believe you told me I was going to muck it up *before the audition even started* – what kind of friend does that? You made me so nervous about messing up that I *did*!'

Freya frowns at me, shakes her head, then leaves.

'No! That's not what I meant!' I tell Belle. 'I was trying to warn you – I swear!'

'Yeah, right, Anni.'

'Belle—'

'Just *leave me alone*!' she hollers, her voice echoing harshly as she races out, slamming the door behind her.

Hot tears stream down my cheeks like the rain streaking the windows. I did it. I saved Belle from embarrassing herself. No one can call her 'Bombshell Belle' today.

But now she hates me for it.

I can't win.

MAX

Ugh. Bunking off has been a total washout! Literally!

I'm soaking wet, starving, and sheltering in a shop full of things I can't afford. I flick through some magazines to kill time.

'*Excuse* me.' The guy behind the counter clears his throat irritably. 'This isn't a library. Are you going to buy anything?'

Time to move on. It's been like this in every shop. I get about ten minutes, tops, before someone hassles me about buying something or asks why I'm not at school. To be honest, I almost wish I was.

At least it's stopped raining at last. I glance up at the clock tower. Five past three – *yes*! School finished five minutes ago and I'm finally safe to head back for the Cup Final! This time we're *definitely* going to beat Farlington. After all, I won't make the same mistakes today – and I know all their tactics! I break into a sprint as I race down the hill, but then skid to a halt as I spot a familiar woman walking towards me: Mum!

I dart into a side street and hide behind a bin. If she sees me I am *so* dead. Even if she doesn't know I've bunked off, we're *never* allowed to go into town by ourselves.

But wait! Why isn't Mum at work? And if she's not at work,

why couldn't she come to my match? I frown. It's too late for a lunch break – is she bunking off too? Weird. Suddenly there's a screech of tyres behind me – followed by a *thud*.

I spin round, and my jaw drops in horror.

ANNI

I can't believe my do-over day has turned out even WORSE than yesterday! Belle hasn't said a single word to me since lunchtime. When I sat beside her in Art, she pretended to be too busy painting to even notice me, then she partnered with Hayley in Biology, and I had to pair up with the teacher. The *teacher*! At least the day's finally over. I slump on the sofa, flicking mindlessly through the TV channels, then the doorbell rings. I sigh heavily. I don't want to see anyone.

But as I open the front door my jaw drops.

'SURPRISE!'

It's Belle!

'H-hi!' I stammer. 'I'm so, so sorry about what happened earlier.'

'Forget it.' She shrugs.

'Really?' My heart lifts.

'Anni, you're my BFF, and it's your birthday.' She smiles. 'I'm not going to let one little tiff ruin your special day.'

'Thanks, Belle!' I beam. She's such a good friend!

'Besides, I'd already organized your party!' She gestures behind her and I step on to the porch to see kids from school waiting on the pavement. *Loads* of them!

'B-but, Belle – I told you I couldn't have a p-party!' I stammer, panicking.

'That's what makes it a surprise, silly!' She laughs again. 'I invited EVERYONE – it's going to be EPIC!'

'Let's get this party started!' a guy I don't know yells.

'Yeah!' Belle cries. 'Woo-hoo!'

'No, no, no, NO!' I scuttle back inside. 'No party!'

Belle's smile freezes on her face. 'Why not?'

'Because . . . I haven't asked my parents!'

'Don't worry! Everyone will be gone WAY before they get home.'

Yeah, right, like yesterday?

I shake my head wildly. 'I'm sorry, Belle, I can't.'

'Anni, this is our chance to be popular,' she hisses, ducking inside. 'If we throw an amazing party, *everyone* will know who we are – we'll be the talk of the school. Don't you want to be popular?'

I swallow hard. *More than anything* . . . except a replay of last night!

'I'm sorry, Belle. But I can't have a party. Everyone has to leave.'

Belle's eyes widen. 'Anni, *please*, that's social suicide – for *both* of us. If you cancel this party now, and humiliate me like this, they will *never* forget it. We'll be the laughing-stock of the whole school.'

'I'm sorry, but—'

'And I will never forgive you,' she warns, her eyes cold.

I falter, torn. But I've been here before, I've seen how this pans out. And either way I lose Belle as a friend.

But I don't have to wreck everything else.

I take a deep breath. 'I'm sorry, Belle, but no. No party.'

She stares at me in disbelief, then turns on her heel and marches down the drive. 'Party's off!'

Everyone groans loudly.

'Don't blame *me*,' Belle says quickly. '*I* was totally up for it. I *organized* it, but Anni's cancelled.'

'Why?!' someone yells.

'Good question. Tell them, Anni!' Belle rounds on me and my heart beats fast. But I can't explain. I can't even speak. There's so many people . . .

'Because she's *scared*!' As Belle raises her voice, Nosy Nora peers out of her open window. Everyone stares at me, their eyes burning like spotlights, and I want to just melt into the floor.

'You're always so scared, Anni – you're scared of talking to people, of making friends, of auditioning, of getting bad grades, and now you're scared of throwing one *itty-bitty* party on your *birthday*? While Max is having the time of his life *bunking off school* all day?' Belle yells. 'When are you going to stop being scared of life and start *living*?'

I bite my lip, tears blurring my eyes.

'Get a life, Anni.' She sighs, turning away and striding out of mine forever.

MAX

Cold terror streams through me as I stare at the old lady lying on the road in front of a white car.

'Are you OK?' I hurry to her side, then gasp as I recognize her. 'Mrs MacCready! Can you hear me?'

She doesn't reply. She just lies there, eyes closed, like she's taking a nap in the middle of the street.

'Oh my *goodness*!' A man climbs out of the car and stares at her, horrified. 'Is she hurt? I didn't see her – I was on my phone – I'm such an idiot! I'll never do it again, I swear, just please let her be OK!'

'Call an ambulance!' I yell at him.

He runs back to his car and returns white-faced. 'My – my mobile's broken!' he wails, holding it up. 'It flew out of my hand when I braked.'

Terrific. 'Stay with her!' I jump to my feet, race to the main road and stop the first person I see. 'Can I borrow your mobile?'

'No!' she snaps, hugging her handbag.

'Please! It's an emergency!'

The next person pushes past me – and the next! This is useless! Then I spot a phone box. Thank goodness you don't need money for emergency calls.

'Ambulance!' I tell the dispatcher. 'An old lady's been hit by a car.'

'Which road?'

'I don't know!' *Why didn't I look?* 'Um, it's the side street off the high street – the one that leads to the bridge.'

'Bridge Street?'

'Yes!' *Duh, Max!*

'OK. An ambulance is on its way,' she assures me in her frustratingly calm, frustratingly slow voice. 'But the lady might need your help before it can get there. Is she breathing?'

'I don't know! I don't think so. I can't remember!' *Why didn't I check?*

'If she's stopped breathing you'll need to do CPR.'

'I don't know CPR!' I wail, panicking. 'What if I do it wrong?'

'Calm down –'

'I'll find someone who knows what to do.' I drop the receiver and hurry into the nearest shop. 'Does anyone know CPR?' Lots of people look up, but shake their heads.

'Try the chemist over the road!' a woman suggests.

'Good idea!' Sure enough, he knows CPR. We hurry back to the side street, where a small crowd has gathered around

Mrs MacCready, and a man is trying to pick her up.

'Don't move her! She could have internal injuries!' the chemist shouts, pushing through. He drops to his knees by her side, checks her over, then frowns. 'She isn't breathing.' He places both of his hands on her chest and thumps her, hard.

'Careful!' I cry. 'You'll hurt her!'

But he just keeps thumping, and I hear him counting under his breath. Finally he stops, lifts her chin, pinches her nose, and blows into her mouth. Then he starts thumping her chest again and I can't watch.

Please be OK, please be OK, I beg silently. Then suddenly Mrs MacCready gasps and starts breathing. YES! But she doesn't open her eyes.

'Is she OK?' I ask anxiously. 'Why isn't she waking up?'

'We've done all we can,' the chemist says, patting my shoulder. 'You might well have saved her life.'

Just then the sound of sirens fills the air and an ambulance arrives, followed by a police car.

'How long was she unresponsive?' a paramedic asks as they hurry over.

'Um, I'm not sure . . .' I falter. It feels like forever.

'About five minutes,' the driver says shakily, turning from talking to a policewoman. 'My watch broke in the crash. It still reads twenty past three.'

The paramedic's expression darkens.

'What does that mean?' I ask desperately as they load her into the ambulance. 'Will she be OK? She will wake up, won't she? She'll make a full recovery?'

'We'll do our best for her, I promise,' the paramedic says, climbing in quickly. 'You did well getting help fast. Every second counts.'

He slams the door and I watch them speed away, sirens wailing.

That wasn't what I asked.

ANNI

She's gone. Belle's gone. Everyone's gone. I lie in bed, the covers over my head, just waiting for today to be over.

'Max?' Mum shouts suddenly, slamming the front door. 'Anni?'

'Upstairs!' I hurry on to the landing, the panic in her voice making me nervous.

'Anni!' Mum rushes upstairs, her face pale. 'Where's Max?'

'I don't know,' I say slowly, cold dread trickling through my veins. 'Why?'

'Drop the act, young lady.' Mum glares at me. 'You know very well that he bunked off school today. Nora called me.'

Nosy Nora strikes again. Of course. She heard Belle yelling at me earlier . . .

'Why on earth didn't you tell someone, Anni?' Mum exclaims. 'I thought you were the *sensible* one! What if something's happened to him?'

'I . . . I'm sorry,' I say helplessly.

'Sorry's not good enough. You're grounded.' She storms downstairs and I glance at my watch. Omigosh, why *isn't* Max home yet? What if something awful *has* happened to him? Hundreds of terrible scenarios fill my head. What if he's lost? What if he's been kidnapped? What if he's hurt – or worse? *What if I never see him again?*

Then suddenly I hear the front door open.

'*Max?* Where on earth have you *been*!'

I sink on to the top stair, dizzy with relief. I don't know whether to hug Max or kill him!

Mum opts for the latter.

'What were you *thinking*?' she yells. 'I was so worried! You're grounded for a month and banned from football. Go to your room!'

'Thanks a lot, Max,' I hiss as he trudges upstairs. 'You've got me in trouble too.'

'Sorry,' he mumbles miserably, slumping past me and sinking on to his bed.

'So? Was it worth it?' I ask, following him, hands on hips. 'Was your bunking-off birthday miles better than yesterday's? You're still grounded and still banned from playing football, after all?'

He shrugs. 'Doesn't matter.'

I frown. Even when Max is in trouble he's usually fired up, ready with an excuse for everything, or shouting about how unfair it all is.

'Are you OK?'

He shakes his head. Wait, is that a *tear* rolling down his cheek? Max hardly ever cries . . .

'Did you lose the match again? Is that it?' *Boys and their football!*

'Match?' He looks up. 'Oh, the Cup Final? Dunno. I'd forgotten all about it.'

My jaw drops. Now I'm *really* worried.

MAX

I tell Anni what happened with Mrs MacCready, and she hugs me tight, then passes me the tissue box.

'Poor Mrs MacCready,' she says sadly. 'And I thought *I'd* had a bad day.'

'Why, what happened?' I sniff.

'Doesn't matter.'

'Tell me,' I beg. 'It might help. I can't shake the image of Mrs MacCready lying on the road, can't help fearing the worst . . .'

She squeezes my shoulder, then tells me everything.

'It's official. *This* was the worst birthday ever,' I groan,

81

flopping back miserably on my bed. Rooney's smile mocks me from the poster on my wall and I shut my eyes.

'What a totally wasted birthday wish,' Anni agrees, slumping down beside me.

'Wait . . . that's it!' My eyes fly open. 'Today's *still* our birthday, right? So we should get another birthday wish.'

Anni frowns. 'What?'

I sit up quickly. 'Another birthday, another wish, right? We've got another chance!'

'You mean, we could wish for *another* do-over day?' Anni moans.

'Exactly!' I cry excitedly, jumping up. 'Come on!'

'No. No way.' Anni rolls away, pulling my pillow over her head.

'What? Why?' I snatch the pillow off her. 'We could stop the accident, Anni!'

'Or we could make things a whole lot *worse*!'

'How could it possibly be *worse*? Come on, Anni – you've had a rubbish day too. If we go back again you could do things differently, and make things better with Belle.'

'How?' she wails. 'I did things differently today and it *still* ended terribly.'

'But we can try again!'

'No,' Anni says firmly, sitting up. 'Haven't you learned *anything* from today? We just need to accept what's happened, take responsibility for our actions, deal with the consequences, and move on.'

'*Move on?*' I cry incredulously, hurling the pillow to the floor. '*Mrs MacCready* can't just move on – she was hit by a *car*!'

'I know,' Anni says sadly. 'But the accident probably happened yesterday too – we just didn't know about it.'

'Yes . . . maybe . . .' I frown. 'But now we *do* know about it – and we can *prevent* it! We have to. You weren't there, you didn't see how horrible it was.'

'I know, and I'm so sorry.' She looks up at me, her eyes pained. 'But we can't keep messing with the past.'

'Just *once* more,' I beg, squeezing her hand. '*Please*, Anni, I need you – it'll only work if we both wish for it!'

'I'm sorry, Max,' she says tearfully. 'I . . . I can't.'

'You *won't*, you mean,' I snap, snatching my hand away angrily. 'Mrs MacCready's badly injured.'

'I know, but—'

'Anni, she might *die*!' I yell, kicking the pillow across the room. 'But you don't even care!'

She shakes her head. 'I *do*.'

'No you don't. If you did, you'd help me save her.'

'I do care!' she wails, her eyes spilling over with tears. 'But we *can't* go back again, Max. It's wrong!'

'*Wrong?*' I shout incredulously. 'How can saving someone's life be *wrong*?'

Anni bites her lip, tears streaking down her cheeks. 'I'm sorry.'

'Get out!' I fling my door open and it bangs loudly against the wall. 'Get out RIGHT NOW!'

'What on earth is going on up here?' Mum shouts, rushing upstairs. I glance at Anni.

'Nothing,' I mutter.

'Nothing,' Anni echoes.

Mum stares at us. 'Honestly, you sound like squabbling toddlers, not teenagers! Anni, get back to your bedroom. Neither of you are to leave your rooms again this evening. Is that clear?'

'Crystal,' I say bitterly, throwing myself on to my bed and pulling my duvet over my head

I just want today to be over.

And to begin again.

DAY 3

ANNI

My alarm clock jerks me awake from a horrific nightmare about a car crash, and I have never been more relieved to hear its jingly tune. But as I sit up slowly, memories comes flooding back and I realize it wasn't just a dream. There *was* a car accident yesterday . . . and I could've helped prevent it. I swallow hard. Poor Mrs MacCready. Maybe I *should* have wished to repeat today again like Max wanted?

But now it's too late. There's no smoke alarm this morning; no burning bacon.

It's a new day. And I feel sick with guilt.

'Are you all right, love?' Mum frowns as I wander into the kitchen. 'You look awfully pale.'

'I . . . I didn't sleep very well.'

'Come and have some breakfast,' Dad says, pulling out a chair for me at the table.

I glance at Max, but he's sitting with his back to me and hasn't even looked round. He's clearly still angry with me. I don't blame him.

'I'm not hungry.'

'I hope you aren't coming down with something,'

Mum says, feeling my forehead. 'Not on your birthday!'

I freeze.

Our *birthday*? *Again?* But how?

Omigosh! Max must have wished *without* me!

MAX

'Anni!' I hurry into her bedroom after breakfast. 'Thank you SO much!'

She looks up from packing her school bag. 'What for?'

'For making the wish after all.' I still can't believe she did it – she's the best sister in the world! *Who knew?*

'I didn't.' She frowns. '*Your* wish must've worked all by itself.'

'But I didn't wish either.'

'Yeah, right.'

'I wasn't allowed to leave my room, remember?'

She raises an eyebrow. 'Like rules ever stopped you doing what you wanted. You're the "fun" twin, remember?'

'I didn't wish, Anni!'

'But . . . but you *must've* done – it's the *only* explanation . . .' Anni slumps on to her bed, clutching her head.

'Oh, Anni!' Mum says, rushing in. 'You're not well at all, are you, love? Maybe you'd better stay home today.'

Anni does look pale – though that's hardly surprising. If *neither* of us made the wish again, then how is it still our birthday? It's making my head hurt too.

'But Mum,' Anni protests. 'I can't miss school.'

'You have to – you must've got that nasty bug that's going round!' I fib quickly. 'Everyone's coming down with it, and you don't want to spread it further, do you?'

'Oh no!' Mum says anxiously. 'You're definitely staying home then, Anni. No arguments. I'll call the school now.'

She hurries downstairs and Anni sighs. 'Why did you lie, Max? Why do you *always* lie?'

'Hey, I'm doing you a favour,' I hiss, shutting the door. 'Can you *really* face another today at school?'

Her shoulders sag. 'Not really, but –'

'And maybe if you're not there, Belle won't audition for the stupid musical?'

She looks up. 'Do you think so?'

'She said she'd only audition if you did too, right?' I reason, sitting beside her on the bed. 'And it's not like you're skiving! You've already done all today's lessons – twice!'

'True.'

'Besides, you need to keep an eye on Mum.' I lower my voice. 'Something weird's going on.'

'Why? Just because she can't come to your precious match?' Anni scoffs.

'She *never* misses my football matches!' I protest. 'But it's not just that. I got up earlier this morning and overheard Mum and Dad arguing.'

'About what?'

'I couldn't hear, but then they rowed again after Dad answered his mobile when he was meant to be cooking the bacon – it would've burned again if I hadn't turned the gas off.'

'So *that's* why the smoke alarm didn't go off,' Anni says slowly.

'But then Mum got even angrier when Dad told her he had to work late.'

'That's not very fair,' Anni says. 'Especially as Mum has to work late today too.'

'Exactly!' I cry triumphantly. 'But Mum *wasn't* at work yesterday afternoon – I saw her on the high street.'

'Really?' A frown flickers across Anni's face. 'Well, I'm sure there's a perfectly reasonable explanation.'

'Maybe, but wherever she was going it's obviously really *important* if she had to miss work *and* my football match, and really *secret* because she wouldn't tell us,' I say. 'So if she goes again today you need to follow her.'

'No way!' Anni protests. '*You* follow her if you're so worried.'

'I can't – Mum would never believe *I'm* ill.'

'Well maybe she would if you weren't such a *liar* all the time,' she retorts.

I roll my eyes. 'Besides, I *can't* follow Mum today – I have to stop the car accident! Speaking of which, can I borrow your mobile?'

'Yeah, right.' Anni snorts. 'After you broke yours?'

'Please, Anni. I need it just in case I don't get there in time to stop the car, and need to call 999 for Mrs MacCready – every second counts!'

'Oh, right – of course!' She hurries over to her bag, then winces. 'No! Belle's got it!'

I jump up. 'Well, get it off her!'

'How can I do that, if I'm too "ill" to go to school?' Anni argues, hand on hip.

'Rats!' I sigh. I'll just have to run really fast. 'So you *will* stay home?' I say hopefully.

She hesitates.

'Max! Time to go!' Mum yells.

'*Please*, Anni,' I beg. 'Just keep an eye on her, OK?'

'OK,' she sighs. 'Whatever. Good luck with Mrs MacCready.'

'Thanks!' But luck's already on my side. After all, we got another do-over day – third time lucky – and without a single wish. Hang on – that's *it*! Maybe it wasn't a *single* wish at all – maybe it was a *double* wish. Maybe because we're twins, and we both wished the same thing, our wish came true *twice*. I grin, just glad I've got another chance to get today right – starting by *not* getting get hit by Jake's football on the way to school.

'Heads up!' he yells, and I immediately duck – but Ben doesn't.

'OWWW!' he wails, clutching his face as blood leaks through his fingers.

Uh-oh.

ANNI

Honestly, Max is so suspicious. Just because Mum's busy this afternoon, it doesn't mean she's up to something. He's spoilt, that's all. He isn't used to Mum and Dad missing his precious football matches because everything always has to be about Max. Ever since we were little he's always been the centre of attention, always the jester, always getting into trouble, then wriggling out of it with a quick joke or a convincing lie. Just because he's a born liar doesn't mean everyone else is.

But when I head to the bathroom I hear Mum and Dad in their bedroom, arguing.

'What are we going to do, Raf?' Mum cries.

'We can't talk about this now, Felicity.'

'If not now, when? We're running out of time.'

I frown. *Running out of time for what?*

'I know,' Dad says. 'But right now I need to get to work.'

Mum sighs. 'You're always at work. Do you really have to stay late? Today of all days?'

'Yes – we need the money!'

I blink in surprise. Are Mum and Dad having financial problems?

'It's not like when we lived in London, Fliss –'

'I know – nothing is!' Mum moans. 'Longer hours, lower wages –'

'It's not my fault I was made redundant!'

What?!

Suddenly Dad storms out of the bedroom and I duck inside the bathroom, my heart racing as he thunders down the stairs.

Dad lost his job? That's why we moved here? But Mum and Dad always said it was to be near the sea . . . What on earth is going on?

I watch Mum closely all morning, looking for clues. After all, if she's lied about why we moved, what else is she lying about? Why *would* she skip work in the middle of the afternoon – *especially* if they're short of money? I feel terrible that she's taking even more time off – losing more money – to look after me. And even though she's lied to me, I hate lying about being ill. I feel sick every time I open my mouth. Which, ironically, probably makes my act more convincing. In the end I pretend to fall asleep on the sofa just so I don't have to lie any more.

But my head keeps spinning. *What's Mum up to? What were she and Dad arguing about? Why are they 'running out of time'?* I hear Mum jog upstairs and I reach for my glass of water while the coast's clear. Then I spot her tablet on the coffee table. My heart beats fast as I pick it up. This is so wrong – this is totally something Max would do – but if there's a simple, innocent explanation for everything, then a bit of snooping's actually for the best, right? And if there isn't . . . we need to know.

I click on Mum's email but – *no!* – it's password-protected. I try a few different guesses, but get nowhere. I sigh heavily and flop back on the sofa. I'm so *useless* at this stuff! What's the *point* in having repeated days if I can't *gain* anything from them? Lying here on the sofa is no more productive than sitting through lessons for the third time!

What's the point anyway? Why *do* we keep repeating today? There must be a logical explanation – but what? I try Mum's search engine, but it just comes up with websites about amnesia, déjà vu and films about time loops. It can't be amnesia or déjà vu because Max is experiencing it all, too . . . I click on a few of the movie synopses, but none really help. In some there's no explanation for the time loop, in others the main character dies each day – eek! – and in others it turns out to all be a dream. I frown. Could it all just be a really long, weird dream? But it feels so real . . . I pinch my arm – OW! I'm *definitely* not dreaming! So what then? Could it really be *magic* . . . ?

Suddenly I hear footsteps on the stairs. I shove the tablet back on to the coffee table and quickly close my eyes.

This time I actually do fall asleep – until I'm woken by the phone ringing.

'Hi,' Mum says quietly in the hall. 'Did you get my text message? I might not make it.'

Who's she talking to? Dad?

'Anni's off school ill, and I can't find anyone else to look after her. No, Raf's working late. Again.'

Not Dad, then.

'Hang on – Nora's car's just pulled in next door; I'll ask her.'

I stiffen. *Not Nosy Nora!*

'Great, I'll meet you there. Twenty past three?'

She's *meeting* someone? This afternoon? So *that's* why she wasn't at work . . .

'No, I haven't told the kids yet.'

My ears prick up. *What* hasn't she told us?

'I'm waiting for the right moment. If there ever is one.'

I frown. That doesn't sound good.

'I'm just worried about how they're going to take it.' She sighs heavily. 'What it'll do to our family.'

Uh-oh. That *really* doesn't sound good.

'I know, you're right.' Mum sighs. 'See you later.'

She hangs up.

Quickly I wipe the frown from my face, but keep my eyes firmly closed, my mind reeling. Mum is definitely up to something – something she doesn't want us to know about. I feel sicker than ever at the thought. Who was she talking to? Why is she meeting them? What hasn't she told us? And what should I do about it?

I could pretend to be really, *really* ill, so she won't leave me? But then we wouldn't find out who she's meeting, or why . . . Oh, Max is so much better at this sort of thing!

'Hello, Nora?' Mum says, and my pulse quickens. She's phoning Nora to ask her to babysit me right *now*?! I have to do something – *quick!*

'Mum?' I yawn and stretch noisily. '*Mum?*'

'Sorry, Nora – I'll call you back.' Mum hurries into the lounge. 'Are you all right, love?'

'Yes.' I smile. 'Actually, I'm feeling *much* better!' I pull myself up to a sitting position, knocking a blue envelope off the arm of the sofa. 'What's that?'

'It's from Belle,' Mum says, picking it up and passing it to me. 'She popped round at lunchtime.'

'*Really?*'

Mum nods. 'It was pouring with rain, too – she was drenched, poor thing!'

Wow. I open the envelope and pull out a hand-drawn card of a cake with thirteen candles. Inside it reads:

'Happy Birthday, BFF! Hope you feel better soon. Miss you xxx.'

And suddenly I do feel better. Because not only does Belle miss me, not only did she make me a card and walk all this way to deliver it – in the *rain* – but if she came at lunchtime, she *couldn't* have auditioned for the musical! It seems this is finally going to be my lucky day.

MAX

Come on, come *on*! I tap my foot impatiently as I watch the classroom clock. My bag's packed, my coat's in my hand, and I have never been so impatient for the hometime bell to ring in my entire life. I've been so worried about getting to Bridge Street in time to save Mrs MacCready that I did even *worse* in the maths test, but at least I managed to sneak my test paper into my bag so they can't record my mark today – fingers crossed they'll think they lost it. And fingers even *tighter* crossed I'll get to Bridge Street in time. I watch the second hand as it ticks steadily towards three o'clock . . . three . . . two . . . one . . .

As soon as the bell rings I'm out of my chair, running down the corridor and sprinting all the way into town. The accident happened at twenty past three. I glance up at the clock tower as I reach the square – five past three! I knew I was a quick runner, but not *that* quick – phew! I lean against the bandstand, panting as I try to catch my breath, then

hurry up the hill, past the chemist, past the bus shelter –
wait, is that . . . ?

'Anni?' I blink, peering into the bus shelter.

She spins round, startled.

'What are you doing here?'

'I'm following Mum, like you said,' she hisses. 'I've had to
lie to her all day about pretending to be ill, then convince
her I was well enough to be left home alone, but *not* well
enough to go back to school – it's been exhausting!'

Poor Anni so isn't used to sneaking around. Or lying.

'You're right, though,' she says, her face pale. 'She's
up to something; something she doesn't want to tell us
about.'

'Uh-oh.' I frown. 'But if you're following Mum, why are
you sitting here? She's going to come round that corner in
about five minutes.'

'No, she's not.' Anni frowns. 'She's in the post office right
now, but she's supposed to be meeting someone at twenty
past. Quick, hide!' She yanks me into the bus shelter just as
Mum walks out of the post office.

Phew! That was close. But what was she doing in there?
She wasn't there yesterday. But then she was coming from
work yesterday – whereas today she's been stuck at home
with Anni . . .

'Better go,' Anni hisses. 'Mum'll be walking faster now
she's running late!'

'But she's still got nearly ten minutes.' I nod at the clock tower.

Anni shakes her head. 'Max, that clock's been ten minutes slow ever since we moved here.'

'What? *No!*' I dash off up the hill, pushing past pedestrians and splashing through puddles. My trousers get drenched, but I don't stop, don't care – there isn't time!

Please, please, please let me get there before it's too late . . .

But as I round the corner my breath freezes in my lungs.

Mrs MacCready is already lying in the road.

'*NO!*' I yell, throwing myself on the ground by her side, my body shaking with deep shuddering sobs. I can't believe it – just a few seconds earlier and I'd have saved her.

If only the clock tower wasn't slow! If only I hadn't stopped to catch my breath! If only I hadn't bumped into Anni! Guilty tears sting my eyes as I thump my fist on the road. *If only I'd worn my stupid watch!*

But panicking won't help anyone. Especially Mrs MacCready.

Every second counts.

ANNI

My heart beats fast as I follow Mum down the busy pavement. Suddenly she looks round, and I duck for cover behind the first thing I see – a lamp post. Terrific.

I suck my stomach in uselessly, but fortunately there are plenty of people moving around between us, so she doesn't notice me as she swiftly crosses the road, waving at someone.

A middle-aged man waves back from the bandstand.

My heart stops.

A man. Mum's bunked off work to *meet a man?* A very good-looking, muscly, blond man . . .

And she and Dad were arguing this morning. *And* she's worried about telling us something – something that will affect our family . . .

I swallow hard. There's only one answer that explains everything.

Mum's having an affair.

Don't jump to conclusions, Anni, I scold myself. It might be perfectly innocent. A business meeting or . . . or something.

I have to find out. I rush across the road and follow them, careful to keep out of sight as they pass the taxi rank, walk through the market-square car park, then climb into a blue Mercedes.

Oh no! I can't follow them if they're in a freaking *car*!

Unless . . .

I can't believe I'm doing this – it's stupid, it's crazy, and it's just the sort of thing Max would do – but this is the only way to find out what Mum's up to . . .

I jump into a taxi. 'Follow that car!'

'What?' The driver turns round. 'Seriously?'

'Yes, seriously,' I hiss, ducking as the Mercedes passes us. 'Quick, or we'll lose them!' But luckily it stops at a traffic light just ahead. Phew! There's still time to catch up.

'Have you got any money?' The burly driver frowns down at me.

'Um, not exactly . . .'

'Get out.'

'But—'

'Now!'

Oh, sherbet! I clamber out of the taxi, kicking myself for not bringing Granny's birthday money with me – but then I didn't expect to need a taxi! I stare miserably at the blue Mercedes as the lights change and it drives off – then suddenly pulls over! The passenger door opens and Mum climbs out.

My heart lifts. Has she changed her mind? Has she dumped Mercedes Man and decided to stay with Dad? I cross my fingers tightly, but to my surprise she turns and looks straight at me.

'Anni Sanchez!' she shouts. 'What on *earth* are you doing here?'

Uh-oh.

MAX

'Call an ambulance!' I cry, racing into the chemists. 'An old lady's been hit by a car on Bridge Street!'

'Oh my gosh!' the girl behind the counter cries, grabbing her phone.

'Where's the chemist?' I look round desperately.

'Mr Clifton? He's just popped to the bank. He'll be back about –'

But I'm already out the door. I sprint all the way to the bank, and – *yes!* – there he is! We hurry back to Bridge Street, push through the crowd, and I hug my arms tightly, helplessly, miserably, *praying* for a better outcome as, once again, Mr Clifton thumps and thumps at Mrs MacCready's frail chest. But although he gets her breathing, she still doesn't wake up.

'How long was she unresponsive?' the paramedic asks again when he arrives.

'Three minutes,' the driver says this time.

'OK. Good job, everyone. Every second counts.'

I slump on to the pavement, swiping away my tears as the ambulance speeds away. Because he's right. Every second counts. And although Mrs MacCready got treatment two minutes quicker today, I can't help feeling I let her down. After all, I *could've* got here quicker.

And tomorrow – when I relive today – I will.

Tomorrow I'm going to wear my watch.

Tomorrow I'm going to run the whole way without stopping.

Tomorrow I'm going to get to Bridge Street in time.

No way am I letting Mrs MacCready get hit again. She won't be unconscious for *any* seconds at all.

ANNI

'Anni!' Mum yells crossly, running over to me. 'You know you're not allowed into town by yourself. Besides, you're supposed to be at home, resting.'

'Um, I'm feeling better.' I feel my cheeks flush and wish I was better at lying, like Max. I listen to the sirens and hope everything's worked out for him today. At least Mum didn't catch him too.

'Anni Juanita Sanchez, did you *fake* your illness?' Mum gasps. 'I can't believe you'd do such a thing! Max maybe, but *you*?'

I shift uncomfortably.

'You are in *so* much trouble, young lady.' Mum's eyes blaze with anger. 'What on earth has got into you? I can't believe—'

'Felicity?'

I look up as Mercedes Man approaches us. Mum glances at him, then swallows hard and suddenly notices several passers-by staring at us.

'Luke,' she says quietly. 'This is my daughter, Anni.'

'Hi, Anni.' Luke smiles, revealing irritatingly perfect teeth. 'Do you need a lift home?'

'No,' I say icily.

Mum glances at her watch.

'We've got time, Felicity,' he says.

'Yes, thanks, that'd be great,' she says. 'After all, Anni's proved she can't be trusted.'

My stomach hardens as we climb into Luke's posh Mercedes. *What about you, Mum?* I want to retort. *Can YOU be trusted? Or are you cheating on Dad?* But I bite my tongue. *Don't jump to conclusions, Anni!* I remind myself. That's what Max would do. Besides, maybe I can learn more about what she's up to on the ride home.

'So how do you know Mum, Luke?' I ask as we drive off.

He looks at me in the rear-view mirror. 'We work together.'

'So you're both skiving?'

'No, Anni, *you* were the only one skiving today.' Mum glares at me. 'And you're grounded. For a month.' She pulls out her mobile and dials quickly. 'Hi, Nora, sorry to bother you, but would you mind watching Anni for a couple of hours?'

'What?' I cry.

'Thanks, you're a life-saver.'

'But . . . but I'm not ill,' I protest. 'And I'm *thirteen*! I don't need a babysitter!'

'Clearly you do,' Mum says tightly.

'But . . . where are *you* going, Mum?'

She sighs heavily. 'Out. I'll be home later.'

That's not an answer. That's not even an attempt at an answer. How suspicious is *that*? And now I'm out of time.

Nosy Nora is already waiting outside our house as we pull up, and I feel Mum's angry glare on my back as I trudge up the driveway.

She'll never trust me again.

But then, can I trust *her*?

MAX

I grit my teeth as I march up our driveway. *I will convince Anni to wish again. I will. I have to.*

But before I can even put my key in the front door, it flies open and Nosy Nora's wiry frame appears, her squinty eyes glowering down at me.

'Come in, then. Wipe your feet,' she snaps. 'I'm sure you've got homework to do?'

'Um . . .'

'If not, I can certainly find plenty of chores to keep you busy.'

'No, I've got homework,' I say quickly. 'Lots and *lots* of

homework.' I hurry upstairs. 'Anni,' I hiss, knocking on her door. 'Why's Nora here?'

The door creaks open and Anni peers out, her deep brown eyes overflowing with tears.

'What's wrong?' I frown, hurrying inside. 'Are you OK?'

She shakes her head, shutting the door behind me and slumping against it. 'M-Mum's having an affair!'

My jaw drops. 'What? That's crazy!'

'It's not! *That's* who she was meeting in town. A man – *Luke*!' She spits the word. 'Can you believe it? She missed work and left me alone at home to meet a man in the middle of the afternoon! Why would you do that, unless you're having an affair?'

I frown. It doesn't sound very much like Mum. 'Are you sure?'

'Yes! She caught me following her, then he drove me home in his freaking *Mercedes*! *And* Mum refused to tell me where they were going. Everything adds up,' Anni cries, pacing the room. 'I heard Mum and Dad arguing this morning – about money, about Dad always working late, and about running out of time . . .'

'Running out of time?'

'I didn't understand that either – until later, when I overheard Mum telling this Luke guy on the phone that she hadn't told *us* yet because she's worried about the effect it'll have on our family! There's only one explanation, Max.

Mum and Dad are splitting up!' She dissolves into tears and crumples on to her bed.

'No.' I shake my head. 'I can't believe it.' I sink down beside Anni, and wrap my arm around her shoulders, my mind reeling. *It can't be true, can it?* My eyes fall on a photo of us all on Anni's shelf. Everyone's laughing because Dad's just fallen off a donkey on Blackpool beach. It's just one memento of so many happy times we've had together as a family. I mean, yes, Anni's a goody-two-shoes, Mum's a bit strict, and Dad's a big kid . . . but we're a family. A happy family. We all love each other. Don't we?

'You've got it wrong,' I say. 'It has to be something else. If Mum and Dad were about to break up, we'd *know* – they'd have told us.'

'Really? Like they told us that Dad lost his job in London?' Anni counters. 'That that's the *real reason* we had to move!'

'*What?*'

'It's true!' she sobs. 'Honestly, Max, they have so many secrets!' She bursts into tears again and I hug her tight, struggling to think of something reassuring to say – usually Anni's the one calming *me* down.

'It might not be as bad as you think,' I soothe. 'There could be another explanation.'

'Yeah? Like what?'

'I . . . I dunno yet, but we can fix this. It'll be OK.'

'How?' she whimpers.

'Because . . . because we know about it now – thanks to you. You did really well today.' I pat her shoulder and she sniffs.

'Except I got caught. And grounded. And babysat by Nosy Nora, and forced to watch freaking horse racing all afternoon. Stupid sport with stupid names – Cotton Candy and Maltese Millions and Shoreditch Maestro – and they were just the winners. It was mind-numbing.'

'There are worse things,' I say quietly.

'Oh, Max!' Anni claps her hand over her mouth. 'I completely forgot! What happened? Did you prevent the accident?'

I shake my head.

'I'm so sorry!' She throws her arms around me.

'Not yet,' I add.

She stiffens. 'What?'

'But tomorrow I will,' I say grimly. 'Or rather, today.'

'Oh, Max, we can't go back *again*!' She turns away from me, hands raking her hair. 'This is *torture*!'

'Anni, we *have* to – we've been given a gift.'

'Feels more like a curse to me – the curse of the never-ending worst birthday ever!'

'But tomorrow's going to be different,' I insist, grabbing her hand.

'Oh really? What makes you think it's going to be *any* better?'

'Because we'll *make* it better,' I promise, taking both her hands, turning her to face me and holding her gaze. 'Anni, tomorrow we are going to have the perfect day. We'll ace the maths test, prevent the car accident, stop Ben getting a broken nose—'

'Ben broke his *nose*?'

'Yes . . . Long story. *And* we're going to solve Mum and Dad's money issues, and get rid of Luke whoever-he-is.'

Anni raises an eyebrow. 'And I suppose you'll win the Cup Final too?'

'The Cup Final!' I groan. 'I completely forgot – again! But not tomorrow. Tomorrow's going to be *perfect* – I promise.'

'I really wish that were true.' She sighs. 'But how can you be so sure?'

'Easy.' I grin, pulling my marked maths test – complete with answers – out of my school bag. 'Because tomorrow we're going to be prepared. For everything.'

DAY 4

ANNI

It worked! It's our birthday . . . *again*!

I beam at Max as we tuck into our bacon sandwiches, glad I agreed to wish with him last night after all. For, thanks to Max pinching Dad's mobile before his office rang, today the bacon isn't burned and Mum and Dad haven't argued once – maybe we *can* have the perfect day!

'Good luck in the Cup Final, Max,' Mum says. 'I'm really sorry, but I won't be able to make it to this one.'

My sandwich sticks in my throat. I always thought Mum only arranged her rendezvous with Luke *after* Dad said he was working late . . .

'Are you all right Anni?' Dad frowns.

'Yep, just full,' I lie, pushing back my chair. 'I'm going to get ready for school.'

'Me too,' Max says, shoving the rest of his butty in his mouth and following me up to my room.

'It didn't work,' I hiss, closing the door firmly. 'Mum's still meeting Luke!'

Max says something indecipherable, his mouth full.

'*What?*' Boys and their food!

He swallows quickly. 'I said you'll have to follow her again.'

'No – no way!'

'You *have* to. After all, we don't actually know they're having an affair, do we? If Luke works with Mum, maybe they're just having a meeting?'

I raise an eyebrow. 'In his *Mercedes*?'

'You don't know where they were *going* in his Merc, though, do you?' Max argues. '*You're* the one always saying don't jump to conclusions!'

I sigh. He's right. Since when was Max the sensible one? 'But I'm rubbish at sneaking around,' I protest. 'I got caught yesterday.'

'That's because you weren't prepared. Here, take my twenty pounds from Granny,' he says, pulling it from his pocket. 'With yours too, you should have enough money to follow them in a taxi . . . wherever they go.'

'Max, I can't—'

'You can! Besides, you won't have to skip school or sneak around this time because you *know* when and where they're meeting, so just get there first and wait in a cab. Easy! You can't get caught!'

I sigh.

Famous last words.

MAX

I hurry to the green much earlier today, but instead of waiting for Ben, I go straight to Mrs MacCready's house.

'Who are you?' she asks suspiciously, opening the door.

Of course: she has no idea who I am!

'I'm Max—'

'*What?*' She twiddles with her hearing aid.

'I'm Max Sanchez,' I say loudly. 'I just wondered if I could do any shopping for you today?' I cross my fingers tightly. After all, if I can stop her going out, it won't matter if I can't get to Bridge Street in time after school . . .

A smile lights up her face. 'Well, that's very kind of you, young man, but I like to pop to the shops every day – the exercise does me good.' She starts to close the door.

'But . . . there's going to be a thunderstorm,' I protest.

'I have an umbrella.'

'And . . . I need to do a good deed – for my Scout badge!' I lie quickly.

'Well, you could mow my lawn after school, if you like?' She smiles.

'Er . . .' *That won't help!* 'I'd love to, but . . . won't the grass be too wet after the thunderstorm?'

'Hm, you're right . . .' She frowns. 'Tomorrow, then.'

'Hey, Max! Happy birthday!' Ben calls.

'See you tomorrow, dear.'

Before I can reply she's shut the door.

Pants.

'So,' Ben says as I join him on the path, 'did you get the football boots you wanted?'

'No, I got a different pair. I think the designer ones were just too expensive.' And if I'd known Mum and Dad were having money worries, I'd never have made such a fuss the other day, I think guiltily. Anni's right – I *am* spoilt. 'Besides, I don't need them – we're gonna thrash Farlington with our awesome skills.' I grin. Our awesome *psychic* skills.

'Heads up!'

I turn swiftly and catch the ball in mid-air.

'Whoa!' Ben gasps. 'Nice reflexes, Max!'

Farlington don't stand a chance.

ANNI

I feel sick as we start the maths test. I know it's wrong to cheat . . . but what else can I do? Even with the answers in front of me last night, I *still* couldn't work out the method for solving those last few questions – they must've covered that topic before we moved here. There wasn't time to look it up last night *and* memorize all the answers before the test, but I'll study *extra* hard to catch up – I'll do whatever it takes – but I *can't* get moved down a set. I glance over at Belle, her head bent over her desk, scribbling madly. *I can't get moved away from my only friend – I just can't.* I take a deep breath and start filling in the answers . . .

'What are you looking so happy about?' Belle asks as we join the lunch queue later. 'You've been grinning all through History – and we were learning about the Second World War.'

Oops!

'Sorry, it's just . . . I got full marks in the maths test!'

Belle stares at me for a moment, then shrugs. 'So? So did I. It was easy. Do you wanna hang out after school? Hey, are you having a *birthday party*?'

'Can't. My parents said no,' I say quickly.

'Lame.' Belle frowns.

'Totally.' I nod. *Phew!*

'Now, what's for lunch . . .' Belle eyes the counter.

Oh crumbs, not this minefield again.

'Anni Sanchez?' A girl I don't know hurries up to me.

'Erm, yes?' I say.

'You need to go to the Headmaster's office.'

I blink. 'What?'

'Now.'

Uh-oh . . .

MAX

Uh-oh. I'm used to going to the Head's office all the time, but when I spot Anni waiting outside, my stomach lurches. If my nearly perfect sister's been summoned too, either something's happened to Mum or Dad, or . . .

The office door flies open.

'Come in, both of you!' Mr Peters, the Headmaster, calls.

Anni bites her lip as we follow him inside.

'Congratulations!' he says, perching on the edge of his desk. 'You two got the highest marks on the maths test.'

Anni's eyes light up, but my insides tighten. I know that sarcastic tone. He's used it on me many times . . .

'So, have you been having help with maths at home? A tutor or something?'

'Yes, actually,' I lie quickly before Anni has a chance to tell the truth. 'We've had a tutor for the last few weeks.'

'Well you've certainly made a radical improvement, if the test results are anything to go by, Max. And you've excelled yourself too, Anni.'

'Thank you!' she says, beaming.

'What's the name of your tutor, Anni?'

'Oh.' She glances at me. 'Um . . .'

I glare at her. *Think of a name! Any name!*

'Um . . . Math-Matthew,' she stammers.

Ugh. *Seriously?* I don't know how Mr Peters keeps a straight face.

'I see. Well, I'll have to get this *Matthew* to tutor my own children,' he says, tilting his head to one side, eyes twinkling triumphantly like an eagle about to skewer his prey. 'I've no idea how you managed to get *all* the answers without showing *any* working-out at all!'

Anni looks at me nervously.

'Matthew likes us to work problems out in our heads,' I lie quickly, meeting Mr Peters's gaze straight on. If I can brazen out Anni's blunder, maybe we'll still get away with this . . .

'Really?' He raises an eyebrow. 'I'm not sure even *I* could've worked out some of these answers in my head. Which method did you use for question twenty-five?' He passes me the test paper and points to a sketch of a triangle with a length measurement missing.

'The answer's ten centimetres.' I smile smugly.

'Did you learn Pythagoras's theorem at your last school?'

'Yes, of course!' Pythaga-*what*?

'Wonderful!' He passes me a pencil. 'Show me your working please.'

Uh-oh. As slowly as I can, I write down the two other measurements, but no matter how long I stare at them I cannot find any way in the world to get to ten. 'Sorry, my mind's gone blank,' I say with a laugh. 'I'm not used to being watched!'

'Doesn't *Matthew* watch you?' Mr Peters asks, unblinking.

'No. *He* gives us space,' I reply. 'It's easier to concentrate.'

He plucks the paper from my hand and I breathe a sigh of relief.

'Anni, maybe you could show me?'

Oh, pants.

ANNI

I stare at the triangle and the measurements until they swim before me.

Finally I drop the pencil and hang my head in defeat.

'I – I'm s-sorry, I don't know how to solve it!' I confess.

'But you did it in the test.' The Head frowns. 'Why can't you do it now?'

My chin begins to wobble. 'Because . . . because . . .'

'Because you cheated,' Mr Peters finishes for me. 'Didn't you?'

I nod helplessly. I can't even look at Max.

'You're both in lunchtime detention for a week, and I'll be contacting your parents.'

Oh no! Hot tears sting my eyes and spill down my cheeks. Mum and Dad are going to be so cross! And today was meant to be the perfect day!

'What I don't understand is *why* you'd cheat.' Mr Peters frowns. 'Max, you're in the bottom set. You must've known we'd notice if you suddenly did extraordinarily well?'

Max shrugs.

'And Anni, you're in the top set; you're never in trouble. Why cheat?'

'Because . . . because I didn't want to get moved down a set if I didn't get full marks,' I admit miserably.

Mr Peters frowns. 'Anni, no one in Year Eight could

115

possibly have got full marks. There are topics on this test you haven't even covered yet.'

'What?' I look up. 'You mean *no one* else got a hundred per cent?'

He shakes his head. 'It would've been impossible!'

'But . . . but . . .' *But Belle told me she got full marks . . .*

My stomach hardens as I realize the awful truth.

Belle lied.

MAX

OK, so today isn't exactly going perfectly, but the most important thing of all – saving Mrs MacCready – I'm more determined than ever to get right.

As soon as the bell rings I'm off, running as fast as I can. I don't stop for anyone, my watch is on my wrist, and I've even got Dad's mobile phone safe in my bag just in case.

But I can't control traffic lights. I glance at my watch nervously as I wait – 3.14 p.m. *Come on, come on!* Finally the green man flashes and I sprint across the road, dodge a woman with a buggy and hurry on up the hill, past the post office, leap over the puddles, and race on past the bank, ignoring the stitch in my side and the burning ache in my legs. *Come on, come on!*

At last Bridge Street comes into view. I round the corner – almost afraid to look – but there she is, standing on the pavement! *Yes!* I'm in time! But only just – for there's the white car heading towards her.

'Stop!' I shout, as Mrs MacCready steps off the pavement – but she doesn't even look up. She hasn't heard me!

Panic zips through me.

'*Stop!*' I yell again, waving madly. '*STOP!*'

ANNI

'Anni, stop!' Belle races after me as I leave school. 'Are you OK? What's going on?'

I keep walking. 'Nothing.'

'*Nothing?* You've barely said a word to me all afternoon. And why did you partner with Jasmine in Biology? I had to pair up with the teacher!'

I roll my eyes. 'Poor you.'

'Anni!' She catches my arm. 'What is your problem? Ever since you went to the Head's office you've been totally off with me. It's not *my* fault you cheated on the stupid test.'

I snatch my arm away. '*Isn't* it?'

Belle blinks, surprised. '*What?*'

I open my mouth to answer, then close it again. There's no way I can explain. And I haven't got time for this. 'Bye, Belle.'

'Anni, wait!'

But I don't wait. I don't even turn around. Because

for once I have far more important things to worry about than Belle.

I get to the taxi rank in plenty of time and wait anxiously, checking my watch every two minutes, my mood lifting as time goes by and there's no sign of Mum. Maybe something's changed? Maybe because Dad didn't have his phone and isn't working late, Mum *won't* meet Luke today, after all? Maybe she's come to her senses?

But no. There they are, heading into the car park.

I grit my teeth. Here goes. 'Follow that car!' I cry, jumping into the nearest cab as the Mercedes pulls out of the car park.

'What?' the driver turns around. It's the same guy as yesterday – of course it is! It's the same time, the same taxi, the same *day*! 'Seriously?'

'Yes, seriously!' I show him the forty pounds.

'OK, you're the boss!' He laughs, pulling off.

So far, so good. We follow Luke's Mercedes through the streets, round corners and roundabouts, my fingers crossed at each traffic light, each junction, praying we make it through in time to keep up, my heart pumping like mad. I've never been in a car chase before, and while I am worried about what I'll discover, I can't help feeling a bit excited!

But as time goes by, and the meter keeps ticking as we head out of town, I begin to panic. Where are we going? Have I got enough money?

Then the Mercedes turns into a car park and suddenly a much, *much* bigger worry takes over.

Why are they going to the *hospital*?

MAX

'STOP!'

As if in slow motion, Mrs MacCready steps on to the road, the white car zooming towards her. I am literally watching an accident about to happen.

Without thinking, I race across the street and push Mrs MacCready back on to the pavement – just in time! The white car whizzes past us and swerves on to the main road, cars hooting angrily in its wake.

I did it! I prevented the accident! YES!!

Mrs MacCready blinks up at me, shocked but unhurt. 'Wh-what are you doing?' she gasps. 'Are you trying to *mug* me?'

'No! I was saving you!'

'*Shaving* me?' She frowns, fiddling with her hearing aid.

'No, *saving* you!' I say loudly, leaning closer. 'You really need to keep your hearing aid turned on – you nearly got run over!'

'*What?*' She gasps, her hand flying to her chest. 'Wait ... Don't I know you?'

I freeze. Does she remember me breaking her window yesterday – but how could she ...?

'You came to my house this morning.'

'Oh, right!' All these todays are starting to merge together!

'Looks like you've done your good deed for the day, after all.' She smiles and pulls a fiver from her purse. 'Your reward.'

'No. No need.' I back away, shaking my head. 'I'm just really glad I was in the right place at the right time.' *Finally.*

'Well, at least join me for a cuppa, then?' she insists. 'I certainly need one for the shock, and the cafe round the corner does wonderful hot chocolate – with whipped cream and sprinkles. My treat!'

'That's very kind, but—'

'Please?'

I'm about to say no, but something in her watery blue eyes makes me hesitate. I glance at my watch. I'm already late for the football match, but nothing happens in the first half anyway, and besides, I don't want her collapsing from shock when I've just saved her life, do I?

'That sounds great.'

Her face lights up and a warm feeling spreads through me as she takes my arm. Suddenly I feel like laughing. Who'd have thought, after breaking Mrs MacCready's window, she'd be buying me hot chocolate for saving her from getting run over? I guess you could call it *car*-ma!

ANNI

Omigosh, omigosh, *omigosh!* Why is Mum going to the

hospital? *Is she ill?* I feel better and worse all at once – maybe she's not having an affair, but what if there's something really wrong with her? *That* must be what she was worried about telling us! And she talked about running out of time!

My heart hammers in my chest as Mum jumps out of the Mercedes and rushes inside. Even before my taxi's stopped, I'm out of my seat, ready to follow.

'Excuse me?' the driver yells as I leap out. 'You haven't paid!'

'Sorry!' I hand him the forty pounds quickly, wait impatiently for my change, then hurry into the hospital.

But she's disappeared.

I look around desperately. The reception area is busy. There are people in wheelchairs, others carrying flowers, an excited little girl with an '*It's a Boy!*' balloon, but no Mum. *Where's she gone?*

Deep breaths, Anni, I tell myself, trying to calm down.

Then suddenly Luke rushes in. I hide behind a vending machine as he dashes up to Reception, talks to the woman, then hurries down a corridor. I follow him, trying to keep up *and* keep a safe distance – which is really hard! Then he gets into a lift. *What should I do?* I can't follow him inside because he'll see me. But if I don't, I'll lose him – and Mum.

As more people get in, I wonder if I should risk it.

Maybe there are enough people to hide behind?

Suddenly the doors begin to close – it's now or never!

MAX

I run down the hill and all the way back to school, the wind in my hair, my heart soaring overhead. I did it! *I saved Mrs MacCready!*

The hot chocolate *was* amazing, and it was actually kind of nice to chat to her for a while – and boy, can she chat! She told me over and over how much I remind her of her grandson Brendan, and must've shown me a hundred photos of her family on her mobile phone. They don't live that far away, but she hardly ever sees them. I get the feeling they've fallen out for some reason, and I think she's really lonely. That's probably why she suggested I could do her chores instead of paying for her broken window, I realize. She just wanted the company. Talking to her made me realize how much I miss my own granny, and how long it's been since I last saw her.

'Maximilian Sanchez, where have you *been*?' Mr Hardy bellows as I rush into the changing rooms. 'The match is half over!'

'Sorry, I wasn't feeling well. Better now!' I gasp, yanking my kit out of my bag. 'What's the score?'

'Nil–nil!' Mr Hardy groans. 'Nick, you're off. Ben, you're back to midfield. He may have missed half the match but Max is our best striker. Don't let me down, Sanchez!'

Nick looks exhausted and relieved, but Ben's clearly devastated. He must've been playing striker, just as he'd wanted – and I've taken it away from him, just as his dad's about to arrive!

'Are you OK, Max?' Ben asks, hurrying over. 'I was worried.'

Typical Ben: always thinking of others.

'I'm fine,' I reply. 'Are *you* OK? I'm sorry I've stopped you being striker.'

'It's OK.' He shrugs. 'My dad hasn't turned up anyway, so it doesn't matter.'

I frown as I lace up my new boots. I'm really glad he doesn't know he's about to arrive. Besides, he'll be happy when we win!

'*Miaow!*' Jake calls as I jog on to the pitch. 'Stopped being scaredy-cat, have you, Maxie? I've been having a little *cat-nap* myself – none of your lot have even come near our goal!' He fakes a big yawn and leans back on his goalpost.

'Whatever, Jake.' I scowl. He has no idea what's coming.

The ref blows his whistle, and within minutes Farlington have stolen control of the ball, passing it endlessly from player to player, as before, until finally their striker takes a shot. But again Jamie's ready for it – and this time so am I.

I know exactly where he'll kick it, so I'm already sprinting there, my new boots surprisingly light and comfortable on my feet as I receive the ball swiftly and easily. Maybe they *are* just as good as the designer ones! I look round and, sure enough, there's Kyle looming towards me, blocking me at every turn. But today I don't mind at all.

'Max!' Ben yells. 'Over here!' But I don't even look over. This is my chance. I take a deep breath, then lunge towards Kyle – and tumble, sprawling, to the ground.

The referee blows his whistle and I grin. *Penalty here we come!*

But as I look up, to my surprise the ref points his yellow card at *me*!

'Hey!' I protest, jumping up. 'He tripped me!'

'That's not how it looked to me.' The ref shrugs.

'Then maybe you need glasses,' I retort before I can stop myself.

His expression hardens. 'One more comment like that and it'll be a *red* card.'

My jaw drops. '*What?*'

'Calm down, Max,' Ben says quickly, stepping between us.

'Ooh, don't get your knickers in a twist, Maxie!' Jake calls. 'Or should that be your swimming trunks? You do know this is *football*, not *diving*, right?'

I round on him, anger boiling in my belly.

'Max, stop!' Ben urges, pulling me away. 'He's trying to wind you up – he's trying to get you sent off.'

I grit my teeth. He's probably right.

'Why did you do it?' Ben hisses as we jog away. 'Why didn't you pass to me? I was free. Why did you *dive*?'

'I didn't dive!' I protest. 'He fouled me!'

Ben gives me a strange look, then shakes his head and walks away.

He doesn't *believe* me? But Kyle *did* foul me . . . didn't he? Like he fouled me before? Or . . . did I fall before he could, because I was expecting it? I frown, suddenly realizing that today my shin doesn't hurt at all . . .

ANNI

I hop inside the lift – just in time! – and cower in the corner, trying to make myself invisible behind a large, broad-shouldered man, my pulse racing.

I keep my head down as we stop at the first floor, and watch who's leaving. Luke stays, but no one gets in, so the lift is much emptier now. I shift uncomfortably, and pull my hood up.

Up we go again. More people get out. Still not Luke. I stare at my feet. Finally it's just us.

'Which floor?' he asks.

I keep staring at my feet.

'Excuse me? Young lady?' He taps my shoulder and my head automatically jerks up and my hood falls down. I freeze as he looks straight at me.

'Which floor are you headed to?' he asks.

'Oh, um . . . the top one,' I say nervously, but he just smiles and presses the button.

My mind races. *He doesn't recognize me!* But why?

Suddenly it clicks. *Of course* Luke doesn't recognize me – how could he? We've never met! According to him, anyway.

Luke gets out at the next floor, and I begin to follow, but he turns and shakes his head.

'This is the fourth floor.' He points to the sign. 'You need the next one up.'

'Oh, right, thanks,' I say, kicking myself as the doors close once more. Now I've lost him – and Mum – again.

But at least now I know which floor she's on.

MAX

OK . . . I take a deep breath as the ref blows his whistle for full time. This match hasn't gone to plan at all – but at least we have one more chance.

All through the second half I've been bracing myself for Farlington's winning goal, but it never came. It's still nil–nil! I guess the fact that I'm playing differently affects everyone else's play too – like the 'butterfly effect' my history teacher was going on about. One small change leads to lots of others. Everything has consequences.

And now it's penalty shoot-out time – the perfect opportunity to make the most of my psychic skills! I can't stop the grin splitting my face as I hurry over to join Mr Hardy and the team.

'Harry, you take first penalty,' he says. 'Theo next, then Ben –'

Ben's face lights up, and he glances at the crowd, where – sure enough – his dad is now watching. I smile. This could be Ben's chance to score in front of him, after all!

'Then Hiro, then Max.'

No! Why am I last? Is Mr Hardy punishing me for my yellow card? I might not even get a turn if Farlington miss twice early on – or if we do.

But the first few penalties are uneventful. Each team scores easily, and it's level pegging at two all.

Then Farlington's midfielder takes the next shot – and Jamie's glove just clips it! We all hold our breath as the ball hits the post . . . but bounces in. *That was so close!*

'Good effort, Jamie!' I yell. 'Almost!'

He smiles and gives me a thumbs-up.

Then it's Ben's turn.

I cross my fingers tightly as he gets into position. *Come on, Ben. Come on,* I beg silently. *Do it for your dad, do it for the team, do it for me* – after all, I won't get a turn if both he and Hiro miss . . .

Ben takes a deep breath, looks at Jake, then runs, kicks and – I can barely look – the ball slams into the back of the net. *Yes!* I race forward and hug Ben, who looks totally stunned.

'Nice one, son!' his dad hollers from the sidelines, and Ben glows with happiness.

Four more penalties to go.

Three more penalties are scored.

Finally it's my turn.

I swallow hard, my throat dry with nerves even though this is exactly what I wanted.

'Come on, Maxie, let's end this,' Jake cries cockily.

'Yes,' I say with a grin. 'Let's.'

I take position, exactly as before – that's the key: do everything exactly as before – until the very last moment. After all, I know which way Jake's going to dive. I take a deep breath, flex my fingers, then run as if I'm about to kick the ball into the top-right corner like last time – then suddenly I twist and strike it as hard as I can at the bottom-left corner instead, knowing Jake will leap right.

Except he doesn't.

He dives left.

And saves it.

They've won. Again.

And yet again it's all my fault.

So much for being psychic.

ANNI

So it turns out knowing which floor Mum's on isn't actually all that helpful – there are so many corridors leading in different directions, and I've no idea which department I need! I glance at a sign: Radiotherapy,

Oncology, General Imaging Unit, Children's Ward, Cardiology, Haematology . . . they all sound so terribly ominous. The shiny lino floor squeaks beneath my feet and a strange antiseptic smell fills the air as I explore each corridor, but I can't find Mum or Luke anywhere and soon I'm completely lost. This is hopeless! She could be anywhere! Great spy *I* am. I sigh heavily, admit defeat, and count the change the taxi driver gave me. Oh no! I've got well under half left! *How will I get home?*

I swallow hard. There's only one way. I'll have to catch Mum at the lift as she leaves. I will be in SO much trouble, but that's got to be better than being stranded at the hospital all night. Just. Plus, then she'll *have* to tell me what's really going on.

I follow the signs for the exit but, strangely, they lead me to a staircase instead of the lift.

'Excuse me?' I approach a blonde girl in a wheelchair slotting coins into a vending machine nearby. 'Which way's the lift please?'

She raises an eyebrow. 'Something wrong with your legs?'

'No.' My cheeks grow warm. 'I'm meeting someone there.'

'Oh, right. Well, which lift do you want? There are three.'

What? 'But the exit's down these stairs, right?' I'll have to meet Mum there instead.

'The south exit, yeah.'

My heart sinks. 'How many exits are there?'

'Four.'

'Oh, sherbet!'

'Cheer up. At least you get to leave!'

'What do you mean?' I frown. 'Are you ill? You don't look ill. I mean –'

'That's the nicest thing anyone's said to me all day!' She laughs. 'I have good days and bad days. Today's a good day. And you're looking pretty good yourself.'

My cheeks burn. 'Yeah, right.'

'You are. You have really beautiful eyes and lovely sleek hair. I can never get mine that straight.'

My hands fly to my frustratingly flat, impossible-to-curl hair. 'But yours is so beautifully wavy!'

'I guess we always want what we don't have. Isn't that silly?' She laughs again: a rich, warm, friendly sound that makes me smile. 'What's your name?'

'Anni.'

'Nice to meet you, Anni. I'm Lottie. I'm twelve – how old are you?'

'Thirteen. Today, actually.'

'It's your *birthday*?' Her eyes light up. 'Awesome! Here.' She holds out the bag of Minstrels she got from the machine. 'Happy birthday!'

'Oh no – they're yours,' I protest, shaking my head. I

130

can't take chocolate from a sick girl.

'Two bags fell out by accident.' She winks, then lowers her voice. 'They always do at this machine. One of the perks of spending lots of time here – you get to know all the tricks. Very useful when you need a chocolate hit.'

I smile. It's hard not to: she's so upbeat.

'Besides, it's your birthday! Presents are compulsory.' Lottie tosses the bag to me with a grin. 'Thirteen . . .' She sighs wistfully. 'What's it like? Are you suddenly super-confident, with boys dropping at your feet, stunned by your dazzling beauty?'

'Hardly!' I scoff. 'More like fainting in horror at the size of my massive spot!' I cringe. Why am I pointing out my own flaws? *Idiot.*

'A spot? Really? Where?' To my horror, she wheels herself closer and peers at my face. 'I can't see one. Are you sure?'

I nod. 'I've got make-up on, so that's probably hiding it.' *Phew!*

'Make-up? That makes spots worse!' she chides. 'Besides, my brother always says make-up's for old ladies trying to look younger.'

'Really?' I frown. 'Belle wears it to try to look *older*!'

'Belle?'

'My best friend . . . I think.'

Lottie raises an eyebrow. 'You *think*?'

'I . . . Never mind.' Why am I telling her all this? I don't even know her.

'Come *on*, I miss school gossip!' Lottie cries, clapping her hands. 'I miss *school*. Ugh – never thought I'd say that!'

I smile, then sigh. 'Belle lied to me about getting full marks on a test.'

'Why?'

'I don't know.' I shrug. 'To make herself look clever?'

'That's silly. You shouldn't lie to your best friend. You should be completely yourself. Otherwise what's the point, right?'

'Right . . .'

'Life's too short to pretend to be something you're not. Unless you're an actress – I want to be an actress. And a singer,' she says excitedly. 'I dream of being in *Chicago* or *Wicked* – your school's doing *Wicked*, right?'

'Yes.' I blink. 'How did you know?'

She nods at my uniform. 'My brother goes there. He's been prattling on about it all week. Are you auditioning?'

'Me? No!'

'Why not?'

'I can't *perform* in front of other people – it's scary!' The moment I say it, I hear Belle's voice in my head: *When are you going to stop being scared of life and start living?*

'Perfect!' Lottie cries. 'You should do something that

scares you every day, you know. Life is not a rehearsal, Anni – believe me. *Carpe diem.*'

'What?'

'It means "Seize the day"! Make the most of every moment. I've got a whole list of things I want to do before I die.'

'Before you . . .' My stomach shifts. 'Are you . . . ? I mean . . .'

'Dying?' She grins. 'We're *all* dying, Anni! But don't look so worried. I just need a new heart. Like the Tin Man!'

I frown. 'When will you get one?'

She shrugs. 'It's gotta be the right size, the right type and everything. Could be tomorrow, could be forever.'

I gulp. 'Forever?'

'Ah, but sometimes forever is just one second!' She winks. 'That's a quote from *Alice's Adventures in Wonderland* – my favourite book.'

'What does it mean?'

'It means you should audition for the musical!'

I laugh. 'Very funny.'

'Don't you like singing?'

'I do, but . . . my voice isn't good enough.' I shrug, hugging my arms.

Lottie tilts her head to one side. 'What's your favourite song?'

I hesitate, trying to think of a cool pop song.

'Uh-uh, you're taking too long!' she chides. 'Come on, be honest! I won't tell anyone. I don't even know your last name!'

She has a point. '"Reflection", from *Mulan*,' I admit. 'I know it's childish, but my mum used to sing it to me when I was little, and—'

'I love that song!' Lottie cries. 'It's one of my favourites too! How does it start?'

'Uh-uh – I'm not falling for that one!' I laugh. 'I'm not singing!'

'But you *have* to,' Lottie insists, grinning. 'It's on my list.'

I snort with laughter. 'It is not!'

'Is so! "Make a thirteen-year-old girl sing 'Reflection' for me on her birthday." Number fourteen – just after "Snog Zayn Malik".'

I giggle.

'Come *on*, there's no one else around, and I'll even look the other way – OK?'

'Lottie . . .'

'Pretend I'm not even here.' She turns her wheelchair around. 'Besides, you'll never see me again. What have you got to lose?'

I smile. It does help that she's a stranger, so even if I completely mess up, it doesn't really matter. I won't see her at school every day; she won't tell everyone; no one will make fun of me. There'll be no consequences at all.

I take a deep breath and close my eyes. Then I peek to check she's still not watching. She isn't. Then, before I even realize what I'm doing, I'm singing . . .

'Beautiful!' Lottie cries, clapping as I finish. 'Seriously, you have a lovely voice, Anni. Now *promise* me you'll audition next time you get the chance.'

'I promise.' I smile. After all, the auditions are already over.

'Awesome. *Carpe diem*, Anni! Speaking of which, I'd better get back before they come looking for me and discover the Minstrel malfunction!' She winks. 'Our secret, right?'

'Our secret,' I promise.

She grins and waves, and as I watch her go, I feel overwhelmed with guilt. She's so confident and upbeat, and making the most of every second, not knowing if she'll ever get a new heart, while Max and I are getting all these extra days, living today over and over again.

It doesn't seem fair at all.

MAX

It's not fair, I think miserably as I slouch home. *What's the point of having a live-action preview of the match if it doesn't help us win?* So much for the perfect day.

135

'Max!' Dad hurries over as I open the front door. 'Have you seen my mobile?'

Oops.

I pretend to help him look, then when his back's turned I dig it out of my bag. Six missed calls – Yikes! 'Here it is, Dad!'

'Thanks. You're a star.' He grins, ruffling my hair as I return it. Then his eyes widen as he listens to his messages.

'No!' he cries, sinking into a kitchen chair.

'What's wrong?'

'I missed a last-minute meeting with a client. A very important, very wealthy client.'

Uh-oh.

His shoulders slump as he listens to the next message and I wince.

'Work again?'

'Worse. Your mother. I am in so much trouble.' He rubs his furrowed forehead miserably, then suddenly his expression hardens. 'And so are you.'

'Me?' Has he figured out I took his phone? But how?

He jumps up angrily. 'You're grounded for a week, young man. So's Anni.'

Anni?

'Where is she, anyway?'

'Oh, she had a meeting after school,' I fib quickly. 'But I'm surprised she isn't home yet. Neither's Mum . . .'

Dad shakes his head, raking his fingers through his

136

thinning hair as he paces the room. 'I can't believe she'd *cheat*.'

'Mum?' I gasp, my heart stopping dead. How does he know? *Is it true?*

'What? No, *Anni*!' Dad snaps, rounding on me. '*You've* cheated on tests before, but I never dreamed *she* would! Did you talk her into it? What were you *thinking*?'

Oh, *that*! The maths test seems so long ago I'd almost forgotten. Another psychic replay that backfired horribly. Wait, *that's it*!

'I didn't cheat!' I protest. 'Neither did Anni – we're psychic!'

'Honestly, Max!' Dad barks, slamming his phone on the kitchen counter. 'And you wonder why we find it hard to *trust* you? When are you going to grow up?'

'It's *true*,' I insist. 'They call it "*twin*tuition" or something – and I can *prove* it.' I hurry over to Dad's laptop on the kitchen table. Time to solve all Mum and Dad's money worries, *and* get me and Anni out of trouble!

'Horse racing?' Dad scowls as I bring up today's live races on-screen. 'Max, stop messing around. You need to take this seriously.'

'I am!' I protest. 'Watch – I can *prove* I'm psychic. Cotton Candy's going to win this race.'

'Unlikely,' Dad scoffs, peering at the screen, despite himself. 'Have you seen his odds? And he's way behind the leaders, look.'

'Just wait.' I grin. I *know* Cotton Candy's going to win – just like I know *all* the horses that will win today – because Anni moaning about watching the horse racing with Mrs MacCready gave me a brilliant idea. All I'd had to do was look online last night and memorize the results – genius!

'What the . . . ?' Dad leans forward as Cotton Candy makes a sudden sprint and overtakes three horses. Then the only horse in front stumbles, and Cotton Candy overtakes him – and wins!

Dad's jaw drops. Then his eyes narrow. 'Nice try, Max. This is yesterday's race, isn't it? Very clever.'

'No, it's not!' I insist, hurrying into the lounge and flicking through the TV channels. 'Look – it's live!'

Dad frowns as he watches Cotton Candy's jockey still celebrating his win. 'But how . . . ?'

'I told you. I'm psychic!' I beam. 'I know which horse wins the next race too. And the odds are even longer.' I hold my breath. *Will he go for it?*

Anni was full of disapproval when I told her my money-making plan last night, but, well, Anni isn't here, is she? *Come on, Dad*, I urge silently. All our money problems could disappear . . .

Slowly his frown turns into a smile.

ANNI

I glance at the hospital clock for the umpteenth time,

panic rising in my chest. It's 5.45 p.m. *Where's Mum?* It took me ages to find the right exit – why are there SO many?! – and I've been sitting fidgeting on this hard plastic chair in this noisy bustling foyer for what feels like hours, my heart jumping every time the lift doors slide open. But it's never her.

Maybe Mum left a different way? Or . . . *maybe she's not coming out at all?* I swallow hard. What if she's really ill and they're keeping her in?

Deep breaths. Don't panic. Think!

Of *course*! Mum *has* to come home, because she did on the last three days! Everything's exactly the same, unless . . . unless something's changed because *we've* acted differently? *Like the butterfly effect* . . . I bite my lip.

Think *logically* . . .

Silly Anni – nothing *we've* done today could have changed Mum's *medical* condition, so she's bound to come home tonight too. *Phew.* But what time? She got back at about 6 p.m. on the first two nights – but Nora called her on both days and she hurried home in a panic. What about yesterday? What time did she get home?

I can't remember. I was too upset, too busy planning for today's 'perfect day' to notice. How ironic. But it was probably around the same time, wasn't it? Which means she must've already left. I've just missed her somehow, that's all.

I hope.

I hurry into a taxi. Please let me have enough money, *please, please, please* . . .

'That's twenty-one pounds twenty, please, love,' the driver says as we pull up outside my house.

Uh-oh.

'Um, I just need to go and get some more money from my mum, OK?'

His smile fades. 'Quick, then. The meter's still running.'

I sprint inside. As if I won't be in enough trouble for cheating on the test and being out late without permission, now I have to ask to borrow money for the taxi! I'm going to be grounded *forever*!

'Anni, love!' Dad beams as I hurry into the lounge. 'Happy birthday!'

'Um, thanks,' I say, glancing at Max in surprise. *We're not in trouble?* 'Is Mum here?'

Max shakes his head. 'She's not back yet.'

My heart plummets. *Oh no!*

The taxi honks outside.

'Dad, could I possibly borrow some money? I'll pay you back . . .'

'Course!' He beams. 'My wallet's on the coffee table. Help yourself – we're rich!'

I blink. *What?*

Then I glance at the TV and gasp. I can't believe Max went ahead with his stupid horse-racing plan! I can't believe *Dad* did! That's *cheating*. But then I cheated on the maths test too, I think guiltily. I grab Dad's wallet and hurry back to the taxi – just as Luke's Mercedes pulls up.

'Anni?' Mum cries, climbing out. 'What on earth are you doing in a *taxi*?'

Uh-oh.

'Hey, don't I know you?' Luke frowns, peering out the window.

Double uh-oh!

Suddenly Dad cheers loudly, his voice booming through the open door. 'We're *rich*!'

'What the . . . ?' Mum frowns, scurrying into the house.

Phew!

I hurriedly pay the taxi driver, then rush inside before Luke remembers where he saw me and I get into even *more* trouble!

MAX

'What is going on?'

I look up to see Mum standing in the doorway, hands on her hips.

Oops.

'Felicity!' Dad cries, racing over, scooping her up in his arms and twirling her round. 'You're home!'

'Careful!' she snaps, wriggling out of his grip. 'Put me down.'

'Sorry,' he says. 'I forgot—'

'Forgot your phone?' Mum says quickly. 'Yes, I realized that when you didn't answer *any* of my calls.'

'I'm sorry. I'm so sorry. But listen – we're going to be rich!'

'What?'

'Max is psychic.'

Mum frowns. 'Have you been *drinking*?'

'No – look . . .' He points to his laptop on the coffee table. 'I've won *hundreds* of pounds.'

Mum's jaw drops. 'You've been *gambling*?'

'No!' Dad cries. 'I mean, technically *yes*, but not really, because Max *knew* which horses were going to win – there was no risk!'

'*No risk?*' Mum's voice shoots up several octaves, her eyes bulging. 'Rafael, how *could* you? Are you *insane*?'

'No – watch!' Dad leaps across the room and thrusts his laptop at me. 'Go on, Max. Show her.'

I scan the list of horses quickly. Banana Split – that's the one. But wait . . . wasn't Rodeo Queen a winner too?

'Come on, Maxie,' Dad coaxes, squeezing in next to me on the sofa and ruffling my hair. 'Prove I'm not crazy.'

'You *are* crazy!' Mum snorts, folding her arms. 'Don't listen to him, Max; this is ridiculous.'

I swallow hard, torn.

'I'm placing my bet now, Max.' Dad grins, typing quickly. 'Just choose a horse. Five hundred pounds. All or nothing.'

'*What?* Max, don't!' Mum shrieks, grabbing my arm and dragging me away from the laptop, so I can't see the computer screen. But I don't need the list. I know it's either Banana Split or Rodeo Queen . . . but which?

'Fliss!' Dad protests. 'We'd win thousands!'

Thousands? My head spins. That's surely enough to solve all of Mum and Dad's money worries. And that's got to outweigh Mum's disapproval of gambling, right? *But which horse was it?* I glance at Anni as she appears in the doorway, but she can't help – she didn't memorize the results like I did. Like I *thought* I did. It's fifty-fifty . . . a true gamble. And if I guess wrong, Dad'll lose all his winnings and Mum'll be even angrier.

I sigh, then shake my head. 'Sorry, Dad. I can't.'

His face falls and my stomach twists. He looks so disappointed. But more than that – he looks desperate . . .

'You did the right thing, Max,' Mum says, rounding on Dad, eyes blazing. 'I can't believe you, Rafael! Do you realize what a bad example you're setting? How reckless that was?'

'Is everything all right?' A man appears in the doorway. 'I heard shouting.'

'Everything's fine, Luke,' Mum says, as Anni quickly ducks behind the door. 'Thanks for the lift. I'll see you tomorrow.'

That's Luke? Uh-oh. It's worse than I thought. I watch

through the window as he ambles back to his Mercedes. He is ridiculously good-looking. And quite a bit younger than Dad. *And* he has all his hair. *And* he's really muscly. *And* he's loaded.

Poor Dad doesn't stand a chance.

Unless . . .

'Banana Split!' I say quickly and Dad's eyes light up.

'Raf – NO!' Mum yells, flying across the room and grabbing for the laptop.

But she's too late.

'Yes!' Dad cries. 'Just in time – they're off!'

Mum's face turns deathly pale.

Anni glances at me fearfully and I look away, my fingers crossed tight as the horses race around the track. I have no idea if I picked the right horse. It was a fifty-fifty chance but it's my *only* chance of solving our money worries, of saving Mum and Dad's marriage, of keeping our family together. All or nothing . . .

'As they round the bend, Banana Split takes the lead!'

'Yes, Max!' Dad leaps up and down. 'Ten-to-one odds!'

But it's not over yet.

'Here comes Rodeo Queen from behind. Rodeo Queen is gaining on Banana Split.'

Come on, Banana Split . . . come on, Banana Split . . . PLEASE, Banana Split! I beg silently, feeling sick and dizzy, my heart thumping painfully in my chest.

The race seems to take forever.

'Banana Split and Rodeo Queen are neck and neck as they reach the final stretch . . .'

I can barely watch. Everyone's silent, even Mum's eyes are glued to the screen, her knuckles white as she clutches the back of the sofa, and my pulse is pounding so loudly I can hardly hear the commentator.

'And . . . Rodeo Queen wins!'

My heart stops.

'*NO!*' Dad howls, slumping on to the sofa.

Everyone turns to look at me, and I close my eyes, wishing the ground would just swallow me up.

What have I done?

ANNI

What has Max done? I stare at him in horror. *He didn't know the winner?* It was bad enough gambling when he knew who was going to win, but when he *didn't*? That's insane! And now he's made everything a hundred times worse.

Mum's bottom lip quivers, then she turns on her heel and rushes upstairs.

'Felicity!' Dad jumps up and hurries after her. 'Fliss, I'm sorry!'

We hear their raised voices on the landing and Max puts the TV on mute.

'What on *earth* were you thinking? You're so irresponsible, Raf! And it's not just the gambling. Your office called this morning – you missed a new client because you didn't have your mobile. And I've been trying to get hold of you all day!'

'I'm sorry.'

'You *never* think about the consequences of your actions – you're just like Max! That's where he gets it from.'

Max's cheeks turn pink.

'And Anni gets her anxiety from you,' Dad counters, and I bite my lip. 'Everything will be all right, Fliss, you'll see,' he soothes. 'I'll sort things out at work, and I'll be more responsible, I promise. And you're right about me setting a bad example to Max – I'm sorry, I got carried away. But you need to stop worrying so much. It's not good for you, especially right now.'

My stomach lurches.

'I can't help it. There's so much to worry *about*!' Mum sobs. 'How do we tell the twins, Raf? How will they cope? They still take so much looking after. Max is so compulsive and reckless – he's always getting into scrapes – and now he's dragging Anni into them too! I wish she'd stick up for herself more. She's so painfully timid and self-conscious. If only she could gain some of Max's confidence and he'd learn some of her thoughtfulness. They might be teenagers now, but they still have so much growing up to do. They need us both so much.'

'Shh, it's OK,' Dad says. Their bedroom door clicks closed, and we can't hear any more.

'Wow,' Max says quietly. 'I can't believe how badly that backfired. Actually, I can. Pretty much everything has today. The maths test. The football match . . .'

I look up quickly. 'Mrs MacCready?'

His expression softens. 'No, that's the one good thing. I stopped the accident.'

'Thank goodness!' I smile. 'Well done.'

Suddenly Max gasps and points at the mute TV. 'It's the man who nearly ran her over! Volume on, quick!'

I click the remote.

'Local man John Smith was arrested for dangerous driving today after causing an accident while using his mobile phone,' the reporter says gravely.

'No!' Max cries.

'Two little girls, aged four and six, sustained broken bones in the crash, but looking at their car they were lucky to escape alive.'

We gaze in horror at the mangled vehicle.

'This is all my fault!' Max wails, crumpling to the floor.

'No, it's not!' I argue, rushing over to hug him. 'It's the stupid man's fault. He was on his mobile while driving – that's so dangerous!'

'I know, but when he hit Mrs MacCready he promised he'd never do it again!' Max cries. 'But today I *stopped* him learning that lesson – so he's hurt two children instead!'

'Max,' I say gently. 'You couldn't have known. Every time we rewrite history, other things are bound to change too, beyond our control. Maybe we can't save everyone.' I sigh, thinking of Lottie and Mum, then take a shaky breath and tell Max about following her to the hospital.

'I can't believe it,' Max whispers, wide-eyed. 'Mum's *ill*? But she looks so normal.'

'I know.' I nod. 'But it all makes sense. That's what Mum was worried about telling us – about the effect it'd have on our family. She's not having an affair. Luke was just giving her a lift because Dad had to work.'

'Of course. That must be why Mum and Dad are worried about money too,' Max adds. 'How will we manage if Mum can't work?'

'Or *worse*,' I say, tears choking my throat. 'Th-that must be what she meant about running out of time.'

'Oh my gosh,' Max gasps. 'You're right.'

I bite my lip. I think that's the first time Max has ever admitted I'm right. And I really wish I wasn't.

Suddenly Max jumps up.

'Where are you going?'

'To talk to Mum and find out what's wrong with her.'

'You can't!' I protest. 'How will you explain how we know she's ill?'

'I . . .' He falters in the doorway. 'I don't know.'

'I'm sure she'll tell us when she's ready.'

'But she thinks we're not mature enough to handle it!' Max paces the room miserably. 'She thinks I'm too reckless.'

'And I'm too timid.' I hug a cushion sadly.

We both sigh heavily.

'But that was the *old* us,' Max argues. 'After the past few days, I couldn't be *more* aware of the consequences of my actions. And you were really brave, following Mum today.'

I smile, thinking of Lottie. 'Life's not a rehearsal.'

'No – but maybe the last few days have been,' Max says thoughtfully. 'Maybe they were our chance to try again, to learn. To grow up. We need to show Mum we've changed.' He swallows hard. 'How long do you think she has left?'

I shrug. 'I don't know. But you're right, we need to set her mind at rest and help her make the most of every moment.' *Carpe diem*.

'Every second counts.' Max nods. *'Mission: Make Mum Happy* is a go!'

DAY 5

ANNI

Carpe diem, carpe diem, carpe diem. That motto has been running round and round my head ever since I woke up and immediately jumped out of bed, eager not to waste a single second of the day.

Then I heard Mum throwing up in the bathroom on my way downstairs and that made me even more determined. Poor Mum.

'Happy birthday, Anni!' Dad calls as he hurries out of the kitchen, fumbling with his ringing mobile phone. I freeze. Max wished without me AGAIN?! *Why?* He already saved Mrs MacCready, he can't stop those kids getting hurt as well! I know we agreed to spend as much time as possible with Mum – but not like *this*!

I march into the kitchen and find him by the stove.

'What on *earth* are you playing at?' I demand.

'Um, cooking bacon?'

'Very funny. Not.'

'What's not funny?' Mum asks, walking in behind me, looking pale.

I bite my tongue.

'My cooking, apparently.' Max shrugs.

'*You're cooking?*' Mum laughs. 'Who are you, and what have you done with my little boy?'

'I'm growing up,' Max says, straightening his shoulders. 'I'd like to help out more and take on more responsibilities. I'm a teenager now, after all.'

'Yes, you are.' Mum ruffles his hair and smiles. 'Thank you. Happy birthday, you two.'

I force a smile. We might be teenagers, but we're not exactly growing up – we haven't aged at *all* in the last five days!

The rest of the morning goes as ever. We eat bacon butties, open our cards and unwrap the same two presents yet again . . .

But today Max looks genuinely delighted with his boots. He jumps up and hugs Mum and Dad and they beam at him happily as I unwrap my top.

'Do say if you don't like it, won't you, Anni?' Mum says for the fifth time this week. Fifth time *today*, technically.

And for the fifth time I take a deep breath, about to tell her I love it, but then I hesitate, remembering what she said about me last night. *I wish she'd stick up for herself more.*

'Actually,' I say tentatively. 'It's not really my style. Would you mind if we exchanged it?'

Mum blinks in surprise and blood rushes to my cheeks as Max glares at me. What was I *thinking*? I should've just accepted it politely like before. Now I've hurt Mum's feelings – and she's *ill*!

But then she smiles. 'No, of *course* I don't mind, darling. I'd much rather you have something you like. You're the one who'll wear it, after all.'

I smile, flooded with relief. 'Maybe we could go and choose something together at the weekend?'

Mum squeezes my hand. 'That would be wonderful. I can't wait.'

Phew!

MAX

Phew! That was close. I glare at Anni. She's never done *anything* like that before! She must've wished for today to repeat again so that we have more time to make Mum happy – which is cool, but why didn't she tell me? – then she pulls a stunt like that and nearly ruins everything. Honestly!

I mean, Mum doesn't *look* upset about swapping the pink top, but what if she's actually secretly heartbroken? I have to do something to cheer her up – and fast.

'Why don't we invite Granny over for tea tonight?' I suggest.

'Granny?' Mum sounds surprised. 'Wouldn't you rather have friends round for your birthday tea?'

'No – we haven't seen Granny in ages, and it'd be nice to thank her in person for our birthday money and cards.' I'd been meaning to suggest it anyway after my chat with

Mrs MacCready yesterday, and especially now that we know Mum's ill. 'What do you think, Anni?' *Don't screw this up!*

'That sounds wonderful!' she cries.

'Great idea!' Dad says.

'What a lovely thought.' Mum smiles, squeezing my hand. 'I'm sure it'll make her day.'

Great! Now to make the rest of ours go perfectly . . .

'Don't forget your mobile, Dad!' Anni calls as he grabs his jacket.

'But don't use it while driving!' I add, thinking of John Smith.

'Course not!' Dad laughs as he dashes out. But it's no laughing matter. My stomach twists miserably, my appetite gone as I think of Mrs MacCready and the two little girls. That's the one thing I *can't* put right today, no matter what I do. I can't save them all from getting hurt, can't stop Mr Smith using his mobile while driving . . .

Wait. Maybe I *can*!

ANNI

I can't *believe* Max made *another* wish without me! We could be going round in this horrible loop forever – unless I stop him . . .

I hurry to the cupboard under the stairs and find the stripy candle. Bingo! If I take it, Max *can't* wish again!

'Anni?' Mum says suddenly, and I spin round quickly,

tucking the candle into my coat pocket. 'What are you doing?'

'I was looking for the shoe polish,' I say quickly. Lies are certainly coming to me quicker these days – though I'm not sure if that's a good thing . . .

'You found your presents!' Mum gasps, shutting the cupboard door quickly. 'Don't tell Max – he'd open them all before school if he found them!'

'Don't worry, I won't tell him.'

'Won't tell who what?' Max asks, hurrying downstairs.

'Never you mind.' Mum winks at me. 'Are you feeling OK, Max? You've been in the bathroom for ages.'

'I'm fine. Love you, Mum.' He kisses her cheek, and she smiles, startled.

'Have a good day, Mum. Love you too.' I kiss her goodbye, then dash out the door after Max.

'I love you both too!' Mum calls. 'Happy birthday!'

'What was all that about?' Max asks as I catch up with him. 'Did Mum tell you what's wrong with her?'

'No, of course not.'

'Then what can't you tell me?' he demands. 'Twins shouldn't have secrets.'

'Hypocrite!'

'I know – I'm sorry.' He sighs. 'But I only didn't tell you because there wasn't time – and cos Mum'd go mental if she knew I was making so many calls.'

I frown. 'Calls?'

'In the bathroom,' he explains. 'I was trying to ring John Smith and prevent the accident, but there were so many John Smiths in the phone book I only had time to call half of them, and none of them seemed to be the right one. When I begged them not to use their mobile phone while driving, they all denied they ever would. Some of them got quite angry, for some reason.'

'I'm not surprised! Imagine if a stranger rang you up at eight a.m. and accused you of breaking the law!'

'S'pose. Hey, aren't you meeting Belle?' Max asks as I follow him towards the green.

'Not today.' After talking to Lottie I'm not sure how I feel about Belle any more.

'Hey, Max, there you are!' Ben cries, leaping on to Max's shoulders. 'Happy birthday, you two!'

'Thanks, Ben.' I smile.

'Heads up!' someone yells, and I spin round to see a ball flying straight at my face.

'Watch out!' Max cries, catching it, inches from my nose.

'Whoa!' Ben gasps. 'Nice save!'

'Practice makes perfect.' Max winks at me.

MAX

'Let me get this right,' Anni hisses as we leave Ben in our form room. 'You, Maximilian Sanchez, want to *voluntarily* go to the Head's office and *admit* you've already seen today's test?'

I nod. 'Look how much trouble we got into yesterday for cheating.'

'So don't cheat!'

'I'm not *intending* to,' I protest. 'But I *know* the answers now – so I won't know if I'm getting stuff right because I know how to do it, because I've sat the test three times already, or because I've memorized the answers.'

'You could just show your working for everything?' she suggests.

'Yeah, but it's easier to work out how to get the answer once you *know* the answer, isn't it? I don't want to get into trouble for *accidentally* cheating – so we need a new test.'

'I'm not arguing – I'm just surprised, that's all.' Anni smiles. 'And a bit proud.'

'Whatever.' I shrug, my cheeks burning as I knock on the Head's door.

'Come in!' he bellows, then frowns at me as we walk inside. 'Yes?'

I take a deep breath. 'It's about today's maths test—'

'Don't tell me,' he interrupts, folding his arms and leaning back in his chair. 'You've come up with an excuse not to take it?'

'No! Well, *yes*, actually. Sort of. We've already seen the paper.'

Mr Peters's eyebrows shoot up. 'You've *seen* it? How? Did you *steal* it?'

'No!' Anni gasps. 'Of course not!'

'Then how have you seen it?' he demands, leaning forward on his desk and narrowing his eyes.

'Um ... I ...' Oh, pants. I have not thought this through at ALL. *When will I learn?* Here we are, trying to be honest, but we can't tell the whole truth or it'll sound like a *lie*. This is so complicated ...

'We found a copy,' I fib. 'We think someone was passing it around the school. Not us!' I add hastily.

'Not another word, Max,' Mr Peters snaps. 'In the three months you've been here you've become infamous for your tall tales.'

Uh-oh.

'Anni, on the other hand, is a model student, and I know she'll tell me the truth about what *really* happened – won't you, Anni?'

He turns his piercing gaze on her and she visibly shrinks.

We're doomed. Anni can't lie to save her life. Or mine. Detention here we come.

'So where exactly did you get the test paper, Anni?'

She glances at me nervously. 'Um, like Max said, we found it.'

'Where?'

'It was, er ... blowing round the playground.'

Mr Peters raises an eyebrow. 'The *playground*?'

Anni nods. 'W-we thought it wasn't fair that some people would have seen it and others h-haven't, so we came to tell you.'

He frowns, then holds out his hand. 'Let me see it.'

'Oh, er, w-we d-don't have it any more,' Anni stammers. 'It, um, blew away.'

Seriously? She is SO bad at this.

'Oh really?' Mr Peters tilts his head. 'So how do I know you saw it at all? That you're not just trying to get out of taking the test?'

'Oh. Well . . .' Anni falters.

Come on, Anni!

'Because we know all the answers!' she says suddenly. 'Forty-two, three, Harriet . . .' She begins reeling them off.

'Wait, wait.' Mr Peters hurries to his laptop. 'Hm.' His frown deepens. 'And you expect me to believe you had nothing to do with this leak, Max?'

My jaw drops in outrage. *Typical!*

'He didn't,' Anni insists. 'Why would we come forward if we stole it? Why wouldn't we just keep quiet – and do really well on the test?'

Like we did yesterday . . .

'Hmm. You've got a point.' The Head nods, and I flash Anni a smile. *She's learning.*

'Well, thank you for bringing this to my attention,' he

says finally, taking a deep breath. 'It looks like I'll have to find another test paper, and rearrange the test for another day.'

Result! I grin at Anni. She's saved the day! No maths test, no detention, and no getting grounded – yet. Who knew my little sister had it in her?

And who knew the best excuse would be telling the (sort of) truth?!

ANNI

'What's for lunch?' Belle eyes the counter.

'Lasagne for me, please,' I say loudly.

'Really?' Belle wrinkles her nose. 'All that grease?'

'*Carpe diem.*' I shrug.

'But you've got to be careful now you're a teenager, you know. In fact . . .' She stares at my face. 'Is that a spot?'

'No, it's not!' I snap. I checked my face in the mirror thoroughly at break-time, and Lottie was right: there aren't any spots.

'Whoa! Sor-ry!' Belle retorts. 'Looks like *someone* got out the wrong side of bed this morning. Is that why you forgot to walk to school with me? I waited for you for ages.'

Yeah, right! She didn't even wait for me when I was sitting outside her house!

'Don't worry, I forgive you – it is your birthday after all, you deserve a lie-in. Did you have a bad night? You look tired.'

'Yes, actually.' I sigh. I was so worried about Mum it took me ages to get to sleep.

'No wonder you've got such horrible dark circles under your eyes,' Belle adds.

I grit my teeth.

'But don't worry, I've got my make-up in my bag and I'll fix your hair while I'm at it.'

'Omigosh, what's wrong with my hair *now*?' I snap. 'Should it be more up? More down? *What?*'

'Calm down, Anni!' Belle cries, wide-eyed. 'Jeepers! Wear it how you like, and eat what you like too, see if I care. I'm just looking out for my BFF!'

But is she, though? Now I think about it, Belle's always pointing out my flaws and 'fixing' me. I used to think she was helping me, but now I'm not so sure. Why would she lie about me having a spot? And about getting full marks on the maths test?

'Hey, look.' Belle nudges me. 'Freaky Freya is singing to herself again. Lame!'

'Leave her alone, Belle,' I warn.

'Wait, what's she doing now?' Belle hurries over to the noticeboard. 'Omigosh, she's auditioning for the school musical.'

'And why shouldn't she?' I demand, anger bubbling inside me. 'Freya has got a great voice and is a wonderful dancer.'

Belle frowns. 'How would you know?'

'Because I've heard her singing along to her earphones, and she's really good!'

'If you say so,' Belle scoffs. 'What about dancing?'

I hesitate. I can't exactly explain that I've already seen Freya do the dance audition . . .

'You can just tell by the way she moves,' I improvise quickly. 'She's so graceful.'

Belle rolls her eyes. 'Oh really?'

As Freya turns to walk away, Belle sticks out her foot and Freya and her lunch-box full of carrot sticks tumble to the floor.

'Yeah.' Belle laughs. '*Really* graceful.'

That's it.

'Just WHAT is your problem, Belle?' I yell, rounding on her.

Her eyebrows shoot up and the whole canteen instantly goes quiet. '*My* problem?'

'Why would you do that?' I demand. 'What's Freya ever done to you?'

'I didn't do anything!' she protests. 'It's not my fault she's so clumsy!'

'You *tripped* her!'

Belle's cheeks flush bright pink. 'I did *not*!'

'Stop *lying*!' I shout. 'Why do you always feel the need to lie and put people down? Does it make you feel big?'

'Anni,' Belle hisses, her eyes narrowed. 'Everyone's staring.'

But I can't stop myself. 'Because it doesn't make you big. It makes you *mean* and *shallow* and *pathetic*. Why do you always need to be the centre of attention? It's so *lame*!'

'I – I don't!' Belle stammers, looking round at everyone watching. 'You're such a weirdo, Anni Sanchez – no wonder you don't have any other friends.'

'I'd *rather* have no friends than be friends with you, Belle,' I retort. 'You don't know the *meaning* of the word!'

I turn on my heel, my heart hammering like crazy, and almost bump straight into Max and Ben.

'Whoa, that was EPIC!' Max grins. 'Who are you, and what've you done with my timid little sister?'

'I don't know!' I confess. I don't even *feel* like me any more. Adrenaline rushes through my veins and fizzes like lemonade in my chest and I don't even care that everyone's staring at me.

'Something weird's going on with you two today,' Ben says, laughing. 'You've gone all kick-ass, and now Max wants to go and revise in the library! It's like you've switched personalities or something.'

'*Max? Revising?* In the *library*? That's like a really bad version of Cluedo!' I laugh. 'Who are *you*, and what have you done with my *brother*?'

Max shrugs and grins. 'We've got a big maths test coming up – and practice makes perfect.'

'Good for you!' I beam, a spring in my step as I head to an empty table. I feel bold, I feel good – and then suddenly I feel absolutely terrified.

What have I just done? I've just flushed my one and only friendship in this whole school straight down the toilet – *and* I've totally embarrassed myself in front of everyone!

Suddenly I remember the candle in my pocket and I'm flooded with relief. If I wish on it tonight I can completely undo everything that just happened.

But wait, won't that make me the same as Max? I've been telling him that he can't keep rewriting history. It's all so confusing . . .

'Anni Sanchez, you are my *hero*!' I look up as Freya sits down next to me. 'I wish I had the guts to stand up to Belle like that.'

My own guts shift uneasily. 'Maybe I should go and apologize. Some of those things I said were a bit harsh, and a bit public . . .'

'But all true,' Freya argues. 'Don't worry about Belle. Trust me, she'll have a new BFF soon enough, just like she did when she dumped me.'

My jaw drops. '*You* . . . and *Belle* used to be *friends*?'

'BFFs.' She smiles sadly, tucking a strand of red hair behind her ear. 'Hard to believe, huh? But she sat next to me our first morning here and was so friendly and confident, I just got swept along. I couldn't believe she'd picked me to be her friend.'

Wow. Sounds familiar.

'But then, I dunno, it was like I was her pet or something. She was always telling me what to do and how to dress. She got really mad when I cut my hair short and she couldn't style it any more. Then when I decided try out for choir at Christmas, she told me I was "lame". She said if I was at choir rehearsals all the time, we couldn't be BFFs any more.'

'Harsh.'

'I didn't think she meant it.' Freya frowns, brushing a bit of fluff off one of her carrot sticks. 'I thought she was just being melodramatic, and she'd change her mind when she realized she was being silly. But then after the holidays you started here, and she didn't need me any more.' She tosses the dirty carrot back in her lunch-box, uneaten.

'I had no idea . . .' I say, flushing with guilt. I cut my lasagne in two and offer Freya half. 'I'm so sorry.'

'Don't be.' She shrugs, tucking in hungrily. 'It wasn't

your fault, and you did me a favour really. Like you said, it's better to have no friends than to have a friend like Belle.'

My pasta sticks in my throat. 'You don't have any friends now?'

'Oh, yes I do – I didn't mean it like that!' She laughs. 'I have loads of friends; I just don't feel the need to have a BFF at my side at all times. I don't need a . . . *crutch* any more. I can stand on my own.'

I smile, suddenly realizing that's exactly what Belle was: a crutch, to prop me up, to hide behind, to stop me feeling alone. But maybe I'll be OK on my own too?

'And thanks for what you said about my singing,' Freya says shyly. 'I had no idea I sing along to my earphones – how embarrassing!'

'Not at all. You have a lovely voice!' I smile. 'You're going to be great in the musical.'

'You should audition too!'

'Oh, no, I . . .' I hesitate, but then I remember my promise to Lottie.

'Come on, it'll be fun.' Freya grins. 'Besides, what's the worst that could happen?'

Um . . . *I could embarrass myself in front of everyone, I could lose Belle as a friend, and be a loner for the rest of my school life.* But, well, I've pretty much achieved all that today already.

'OK, why not?' I grin. '*Carpe diem.*'

But as we enter the dance studio later, my courage wavers. I forgot how many people were auditioning. My heart pounds as I glance round at everyone else as we do the animal bit, desperate not to embarrass myself. *What creature should I be this time?* Idris is a tiger, prowling round the room, while George is a monkey, leaping around, limbs waving everywhere. Freya oinks and snuffles at my feet, making me giggle, and suddenly I relax. Somehow, without Belle here watching me, it's easier. I could be a hippo – or an elephant, I suppose? I dangle my arm in front of my face experimentally and Freya snorts with laughter, but not in a nasty way.

As the music gets faster I pick up my pace till I'm stampeding around the room, my 'trunk' waving around wildly from side to side. It's actually quite fun. I even steal a pretend banana from George, who then mimes hurling bananas at me, which I catch in my imaginary trunk! For a guy who's so good-looking, he's wonderfully goofy too! Soon I'm interacting with heaps of different animals, and it's the most fun I've had in ages – like being a little kid again – and suddenly it doesn't matter that I don't know these people or would never dream of speaking to them in class or at lunchtime. We're all having a good time together.

Even the dance audition goes much better. I

concentrate hard as the moves start to get more complicated, but now I'm not distracted by Belle, I find myself really enjoying it. I love the feeling of being in sync with everyone else, moving together as a team.

'Wonderful!' Ms Davis beams at us all. 'We have some very talented dancers in this room. Now for the singing audition.'

Uh-oh.

'First up, Anni Sanchez.'

Double uh-oh!

'Go on, Anni.' Freya nudges me forward. 'You can do it.'

I swallow hard, my throat dry as sandpaper as I reach the front. This isn't like singing in front of Lottie at all. These aren't strangers watching – I see them every day! What if I make a complete fool of myself? I'll never live it down! I glance towards the door, think about making a run for it, but Freya smiles at me encouragingly, then George gives me a thumbs-up and I remember his monkey antics. And there's the penguin girl, and Idris the tiger – and suddenly they're all just animals and don't seem so scary any more.

When are you going to stop being scared of life and start living? Belle's voice echoes in my ears and my stomach hardens.

Today. That's when.

After all, if it all goes wrong, I've still got the magic candle . . .

I take a deep breath and begin to sing, losing myself in Mulan's story, in her frustration at having to pretend to be something she's not, her longing to truly be herself. It could be *my* story . . .

Suddenly everyone's clapping and I'm jerked back to reality. My cheeks blaze, but this time it's not from fear or embarrassment.

It's pride.

MAX

Practice makes perfect indeed! Today went SO much better – no maths test, and no detention! I race into town, feeling lighter than air, *knowing* I'm going to make it to Bridge Street in time to save Mrs MacCready – because I did *yesterday!*

Except . . . except yesterday, by saving her, the two kids got hurt instead. My pace slows as my heart sinks. What if I didn't get through to the right John Smith this morning? *What should I do?* This is worse than hearing about the little girls last night. Worse even than not getting to Mrs MacCready in time – because now it's all in my hands. Anni's right: I can't save everyone. Someone's going to get hurt . . . but *who? How can I possibly choose?*

I lean against a wall, my head whirling painfully. What if I was never *supposed* to interfere? After all, on my *first* thirteenth birthday – four days ago – I didn't even know about the accident. Maybe I shouldn't have changed anything. Maybe I should just head back to school and go to the football match as if it were a normal day, as if we'd never had any repeats at all . . .

But I can't just let Mrs MacCready get hurt! What if I've been given these repeated days precisely because I'm *meant* to change things? This is so confusing! So much for Mum saying I never think through the consequences of my actions – it's all I *can* do. If only there was a way to stop both Mrs MacCready *and* the girls getting hurt, to stop John Smith before he hurts *anybody*.

That's it! I'll stop his car before he hits Mrs MacCready. I'll stand in the middle of the road if I have to – that way he *can't* hit her. And hopefully if I'm loud enough and jump up and down he'll stop before hitting me either!

But if he doesn't . . . well, I can just wish to restart the day again tomorrow.

Or hope that Anni does, if I can't . . .

ANNI

'Anni, wait!' Freya calls as I hurry out of school. 'Don't you want to check the noticeboard to see if we got into the musical?'

'Can't – got to dash. Good luck!' I reply, racing to the phone box at the end of the road to call a taxi.

Besides, it doesn't really matter if I got a role or not. That wasn't the point. The point was, I faced my fears, seized the day, and kept my promise to Lottie. Best of all, I've found a great new friend. I partnered with Freya in Biology this afternoon too, and I have never giggled so much! Poor Belle had to team up with the teacher again, but Freya's right, she'll have found herself a new pet – I mean BFF – in no time. Or maybe she won't. Maybe she'll learn to stand on her own as well?

The taxi takes me straight to the hospital today, and I've raided my piggy bank so I should have plenty of money, and be there well before Mum and Luke. I hurry straight up to the fourth floor and position myself behind a vending machine to wait. Each time the lift doors open my heart hammers – this is terrible for my nerves! Then suddenly, finally, Mum rushes out and disappears down a corridor. But I stay hidden, waiting for Luke. After all, it's much easier to follow someone who won't recognize you!

I follow him quickly down one corridor, then another. We hurry past Radiology and the Children's Ward – that must be where Lottie is – until finally he enters a waiting area, and I stop short as I spot Mum sitting inside. I look up at the sign over the doorway: *Early Pregnancy Unit*.

Oh. My. Gosh! Mum's *pregnant*? She *isn't* ill! This is AMAZING! Dizzy with relief, I peep through the doorway to see Mum and Luke talking to each other fervently – and suddenly I freeze.

What if *Luke's* the father?

MAX

Pain burns in my legs as I race up the hill. *Please let me get there in time, please, please, please.*

At last I round the corner, almost afraid to look, but there's Mrs MacCready – crossing the road.

'STOP!' I yell, lunging forward, but I'm too late. The car hits her, and almost in slow motion, she topples to the ground.

'*NO!*' I cry, flinging myself down by her side. 'No! Not today!'

But she doesn't reply. She just lies there, her eyes closed, and it's all my fault. If I hadn't hesitated I could've saved her.

But maybe I still can . . .

'Oh my *goodness!*' Mr Smith wails. 'Is she hurt?'

'You shouldn't have been on your phone!' I snap as I fumble through Mrs MacCready's handbag and pull out her mobile.

'Hey – what are you doing?' he cries. 'Thief!'

'Quiet!' I yell, dialling 999 then putting it on loudspeaker as I start CPR. I quickly explain what's happened, and the lady talks me through what to do. I spent all lunchtime studying CPR in the library just in case – but it's reassuring having her voice guiding me through it.

'Place the heel of one hand in the middle of the lady's chest, place your other hand on top and interlock your fingers. Keep your elbows straight, and use your whole body weight to push straight down, as hard as you can, at least five centimetres.'

'*Five centimetres?*' I gasp. 'What if I hurt her?'

'You need to reach her heart or it won't do any good – now push hard and fast.'

I do as I'm told, even though it feels far too rough for Mrs MacCready's frail body.

'Am I doing it fast enough?' I puff.

'Do you know the song "Staying Alive"?'

'The one by those brothers with high voices?'

'That's the one.' She chuckles. 'Try pushing to the rhythm of that.'

I do, and my pace increases. 'Staying Alive'? How appropriate. Let's hope it works.

'Should I do rescue breaths after every thirty compressions?' I pant, remembering the chemist's actions.

'No, that's only if you're trained – it's more important to get her heart going. The ambulance should be there very soon.'

I hope so. My arms are killing me but I keep going. Every second counts . . .

Suddenly Mrs MacCready takes a big gulp of air!

'She's breathing,' I cry, stunned. 'She's alive!' My heart soars as sirens fill the air.

'Gasping or breathing normally?' the dispatcher asks urgently.

'Um . . .'

'If she's just gasping, keep going, Max.'

'I think she's breathing normally – but the ambulance is here now,' I pant as it rounds the corner and pulls over.

'Well done, Max!' the dispatcher cries. 'The paramedics will take over now.'

I did it! I saved her! I saved Mrs MacCready *and* the kids! As the paramedics rush to her side, I sink down on to the pavement, suddenly dizzy with relief and utterly exhausted by this never-ending birthday!

ANNI

Mum's not dying, that's the main thing, I tell myself, leaning against the wall and taking a deep breath. Mum's not even *ill*. Anything else we can cope with – even an affair – as long as she's OK.

Suddenly she dashes out of the waiting room and rushes straight past me, into the toilets.

Phew, that was close! I turn and hurry away down the corridor so she won't see me when she comes out.

But suddenly I stop. For as much as I hate getting into trouble, it's more important to find out what's really

173

going on. I have to know the truth, whatever it is. That's the only way we can move forward. I take a deep breath, turn round, and follow her into the ladies.

'Hello, love,' Mum says from inside a cubicle, and I freeze. How does she know it's me?

'I'm at the hospital,' she continues. 'No, everything's fine, they're just running a bit late.'

She must be on the *phone*, I realize with relief.

'I just – I wish you were here, Raf. It's your baby too.'

It's *Dad's* baby! Thank goodness! It's all I can do to stop myself squealing with delight.

'No, it's fine, really. I know you'd be here if you could.' Mum sighs. 'I'm sorry about our argument this morning. You're right – you need to take all the hours you can get. Goodness knows we need the money.' She sighs again. 'I know, I know, you always say everything's going to be fine, but what if it's not? We're both so much older now, and how will we cope without my salary? We can't afford childcare.'

So *that's* why they were worried about money.

'And what about the twins?'

My ears prick up.

'How will they cope? It'll be such a big change for them, and they're really still children themselves. Max was very sweet this morning, though, wasn't he? Cooking breakfast and saying he wants to help out more. And

I was so pleased Anni suggested replacing her top – I think it's the first time I've ever seen her stand up for herself. Good for her.'

I smile.

'Yes, maybe you're right,' Mum continues. 'Maybe they *are* growing up.'

'Felicity?' Luke's voice calls from the corridor. 'They're ready for you!'

'Coming,' Mum replies. 'Got to go, love. See you later.'

I swallow hard, ready to confront her, to comfort her, to tell her Max and I would *love* to have a little brother or sister, that we're mature and responsible and we'll help with the baby . . .

But at the last second I dive into a cubicle and slam the door shut. After all, if she discovers I've followed her to the hospital, that *might* kind of undermine my claim of being mature . . .

We'll just have to *show* her instead.

I can't wipe the grin off my face as I hurry back to the lifts. I want to skip down the corridor and hug everyone I see. I'm going to be a *big sister*! Looks like we won't be needing the magic candle again after all.

And suddenly I know just what to do with it.

MAX

As the paramedics carry Mrs MacCready into the ambulance,

175

she blinks up at me. 'Thank you, young man. How can I ever repay you?'

'No need!' I beam, squeezing her hand. 'Just get well soon. And if you fancy a cuppa sometime, when you're feeling better, I know a cafe that does the *best* hot chocolate. My treat.'

She smiles. 'You're on.'

'Can I go to the hospital with her?' I ask as the paramedic shuts the doors.

'Sorry, mate – family only.' He pats me on the shoulder. 'You did an amazing job, though. Thanks to you, she should make a full recovery.'

A full recovery! *Yes!*

'Well done, lad.' Mr Smith gives me a watery smile as the ambulance drives away. He's still white as a sheet, sitting on the kerb. 'You're a hero. I don't know what I'd have done if she . . . if you hadn't been here. I'd never have forgiven myself.'

Me neither, I think. 'I just wish I could've gone with her. She's all alone.'

'Family only.' He shakes his head. 'What a stupid rule.'

I sigh. 'And her family don't even know what's happened.'

'Well, why don't you call them?' he says. 'You've got her mobile.'

Duh, Max! I totally forgot! Quickly I scroll through her contacts till I reach the name Brendan. Didn't she say I looked like her grandson Brendan?

I click the name quickly, crossing my fingers that he picks up as a police car rounds the corner.

'It was my fault,' Mr Smith says, walking over to meet the police officers. 'I'm so sorry; it was all my fault.'

Suddenly I feel bad for him. Of course he shouldn't have been driving while on his phone, but he's so upset and ashamed about what's happened, I know he'll never do it again.

'Hi, Nan!' a boy's voice cries from the phone. 'How are you?'

I take a deep breath and begin to explain.

ANNI

'*Happy un-birthday to you, happy un-birthday to you, happy un-birthday, dear Lottie, happy un-birthday to you!*' I sing along to Granny's musical badge as I hurry up to Lottie's bed, carrying a chocolate muffin from the vending machine.

Her eyes widen. 'But it's not my birthday!'

'No – it's your *un*-birthday!' I explain. 'Like in—'

'*Alice's Adventures in Wonderland*!' she cries. 'That's my favourite book!'

I grin. She gets it – I hoped she would.

'But who are you?'

Oops. I forgot that she wouldn't remember me.

I must seem like a total weirdo!

'I'm . . . the un-birthday fairy – AKA Anni,' I say quickly. 'Here to brighten your day!'

'Well, you certainly have!' She beams. 'Did my brother put you up to this?'

'Who?'

'My brother – he goes to your school.' She nods at my uniform. 'He's always doing stuff like this.'

'Oh no, not this time – pure un-birthday magic!' I do a twirl and she giggles.

'Thank you.' She unwraps the muffin and goes to take a big bite.

'Wait!' I cry, pulling the candle from my coat pocket. 'You need to make a wish first! Make sure it's a good one!'

I wedge the candle into the muffin and we ask a nurse to light it, then Lottie takes a deep breath, closes her eyes, and blows it out – then bursts out laughing as it relights itself.

I'd forgotten it did that.

'Make another wish!' I urge and she blows it out again.

'I'll have ticked off my entire wish-list at this rate!' Lottie laughs as the candle relights itself a third time, then a fourth. 'I'm running out of puff!'

Finally the candle goes out in a plume of wispy smoke, and Lottie grins. 'I hope it worked!'

I beam at her. *Me too.*

After all, if anyone deserves a wish to come true, it's Lottie.

MAX

'Maximilian Sanchez, where have you *been*?' Mr Hardy bellows as I rush into the changing rooms.

Again I apologize, and again he tries to make me striker.

'No, sir,' I say quickly. 'I think Ben should be striker. He's a great goal-scorer.'

'Really?' Ben's eyes light up. 'Thanks, Max!'

'Ben's a better midfielder,' Mr Hardy argues. 'And we need to score – quickly.'

'But sir, Ben deserves a chance to prove himself.'

'He's had the whole first half,' the coach snaps. 'But it's still nil–nil!'

'It's OK, Max,' Ben says, tugging my sleeve. 'My dad hasn't turned up, so it doesn't matter anyway.'

'But . . .' *He's just about to!*

'Who's the coach, Sanchez – me or you?' Mr Hardy says crossly.

'You, sir.' I sigh.

'Exactly. And I want to see you running extra fast out there after missing the first half!'

I sigh and hurry on to the pitch, my legs already aching from running into town and back, my arms still hurting from doing CPR. But I'm pumped up too.

'Miaow!' Jake calls.

'Aw, are you a poor little *scaredy-cat*, Jakey?' I instantly reply, and he stares at me, stunned that I've stolen his line. 'What's the matter?' I grin. '*Cat* got your tongue? Is that cos you've got a *cat in hell*'s chance of winning this match?'

'Whatever.' He scowls.

'Come on, don't be a *sourpuss!*' I retort and everyone laughs. *Result!*

The ref blows the whistle for the second half, and this time I quickly pass the ball to Ben. But – *no!* – Ben's too busy grinning at his dad and misses it! Yet again Farlington gain control of the ball, and yet again they retain possession for most of the half, passing it endlessly back and forth. Finally, with minutes to go, they take the shot I'm expecting – and sure enough, good old Jamie catches it easily and boots it back down to our end where I'm ready and waiting. I chip the ball round a couple of defenders and then there he is – Kyle – looming towards me. What on earth should I do this time?

'Max!' Ben yells. 'Over here!' Just like before, he's on the far side of the pitch, running towards the goal, unmarked.

I hesitate. He fluffed the last pass, but he was distracted. And everyone deserves a second chance. I know that better than anyone – after all, I've had *five* chances just to try to do today right!

I take a deep breath and lob the ball over to Ben, who

pounces on it, and sprints towards the goal. He dodges one defender, two, then feints right and boots it into the bottom-left corner – just beyond Jake's grasp. *YES!* I leap off the ground and punch the air. He *did* it! Ben scored! I race over and throw my arms around him as the crowd goes wild.

'Did it go in?' Ben asks, dazed. 'Did it really go in?'

I laugh as the final whistle blows. 'Mate, you just won the match! The *Cup*!' I ruffle his hair. 'You're our *hero*!'

'Well done, Ben, great job!' Mr Hardy cries, running over as the rest of the team crowd around us, whooping loudly.

I grin as I spot Ben's dad jumping up and down, cheering madly, his coat flapping open. And for the first time, underneath, I spot his army uniform.

My stomach flips. I had no idea Ben's dad was in the army! I've only met him a couple of times, but Ben's my best mate – I *should've* known; I should've *asked*. No wonder his dad doesn't make it to many matches, and no wonder it meant so much to Ben to be striker today. I look back at him, his cheeks pink with pride, an enormous smile lighting his face as Jamie and Harry lift him on to their shoulders, and I couldn't be happier if I'd scored the winning goal myself. Ben deserves this moment. And he deserves a better best mate. From now on, I'm going to be there for him, like he's always there for me.

'Be-en! Be-en!' I yell at the top of my lungs, and soon the

whole team's chanting with me – then the whole crowd!

Except Farlington, of course. I look round for Jake, eager to see his disappointment, but I'm surprised to spot him walking towards me.

'Good match, Max. Well played.' He holds out his hand.

'Thanks, Jake.' I smile, shaking it. Maybe he's not so bad, and maybe hitting me with his ball each morning *was* an accident after all.

'Yeah, well played, Max,' a familiar voice says from behind me.

'Anni?' I wheel round. 'What are you doing here? You're supposed to be finding out what's wrong with Mum!'

'I did.' She leans forward and whispers in my ear, and my jaw drops.

'Are you sure? I mean, aren't they too *old*?'

Anni laughs. 'Obviously not!'

'Wow!' I cry, dizzy with relief for the second time today. 'I can't believe we got it so wrong! No divorce, no illness. I'm so happy, even the thought of stinky nappies doesn't seem so bad!'

'They can't smell any worse than your sweaty football kit!' Anni retorts, wrinkling her nose and grinning. 'Just think, you'll soon have a little brother or sister to play football with!'

'Or maybe both!' I say, laughing. 'They say twins run in families, after all!'

ANNI

The moment Dad's key turns in the lock, Max and I race to the front door.

'Granny!' we cry in unison.

'Twins!' Granny beams, her eyes twinkling with delight. 'Goodness me, you both look so *old*!'

So does she. Her wrinkles seem to have got deeper since the last time we saw her. When was that? *Christmas?* That was *months* ago.

'Thank you so much for our cards and birthday money,' Max says. 'It was really kind of you.'

'Kind, shmind!' Granny scoffs. 'What else am I going to do with all my money? You'll get it when I pop my clogs, after all!'

'Granny!' I squeal, but Max snorts with laughter. I'd forgotten how funny she is.

'Would you like a cup of tea?' I ask, as she bustles into the lounge.

'Tea?' She frowns. 'I thought this was a *party*? Haven't you got any champagne? Or sherry?'

'One sherry coming up.' Dad chuckles, disappearing into the kitchen.

'Mother!' Mum cries, hurrying down the stairs.

'Hello, darling.' Granny hugs her. 'The house is looking very tidy these days. Have you finally taken my advice and hired a cleaner?'

I try to hide my smile. Mum's not exactly known for her neatness.

'No, the twins tidied up before I got home today.' She smiles. '*And* they're cooking dinner!'

I beam at Max. So far, so good.

'On their *birthday*?' Granny's eyebrows shoot up.

'I know, it's a miracle!' Mum beams at us as she takes Granny's coat into the hall.

'No such thing as miracles, in my experience,' Granny whispers, winking at us. 'No teenager willingly cleans the house unless they're up to something. What have you done? Got into trouble at school? Broken something? I won't tell, I promise!'

'I, um, I'd better just go and check on the food,' I say, dashing out and leaving Max to answer. I may be better at lying now, but I still hate doing it.

'That paella smells wonderful, darling.' Dad smiles as I hurry into the kitchen. 'And thanks for cleaning, too.'

'No problem.' I smile back. 'Like Max said, we want to help out more. We're teenagers now, after all.'

'You're amazing, that's what you are.' Dad kisses my head.

'Ah, there's my sherry!' Granny cries, walking in. 'Lovely. Max is just telling us all about his football match.'

'Did he win?' Dad says excitedly. 'No, don't tell me! I want to hear all about it!' He rushes out of the room.

'Coming, Anni?' Granny asks.

'No, I watched it,' I explain, taking lettuce and tomatoes out of the fridge. 'Besides, I need to make the salad.'

'I'll help you.'

'Oh no, you go and relax.'

'Pah! I can relax when I'm dead,' Granny scoffs, and I laugh. 'Besides, I bet you don't know how to make a tomato rose, do you?'

'Um, no!'

She tuts. 'What do they teach you at school these days?' She winks, picking up a knife and setting to work. 'How is school?'

'Oh, OK.' I smile. 'I auditioned for the school musical today.'

'Did you?' Granny looks pleased. 'Good for you! And how's that friend of yours? Belle, isn't it?'

'Oh, she's . . . she's not really my friend any more actually,' I say quietly.

'Really? Why's that?'

I sigh. 'She just kept putting me down. And she tells lies! She lied about me having a spot, and about getting full marks on the maths test.'

'Oh dear.' Granny frowns. 'She sounds a bit insecure.'

'Insecure? *Belle?*' I laugh. 'No way. She's beautiful and brilliant and confident and so cool!'

'And how many friends does she have?'

185

'Well . . . just me, I suppose.' I frown as I wash the lettuce. 'But I don't think she actually likes me, not really. It's like nothing I ever did was good enough for her. You're supposed to be able to be yourself with your best friend, right? They're supposed to like you just as you are?'

'Yes,' Granny nods. 'But it sounds like Belle might be a bit afraid to be herself. Otherwise, why would she lie about doing well? And maybe she criticized you just to make herself feel better? Not that that's any excuse.'

I frown.

'I may be wrong . . .' Granny shrugs. 'But don't throw any friendship away lightly. You can never have too many friends, Anni. Believe me. The world can be a lonely place.' She hands me a beautiful tomato rose, smiles, then squeezes my shoulder as she heads back into the lounge.

I bite my lip. Is Granny right? I feel like I did the right thing standing up to Belle – especially after what Freya told me – but what if we're both wrong about her? And I do feel bad about the way I ended things so publicly.

I take a deep breath, pick up the phone and dial Belle's number.

'Hello?' A woman's voice answers sharply.

'Hi, is that Belle's mum?' I've never spoken to her before.

'Yes. Why? Is she in trouble?'

'No, no – I'm . . . a friend from school.' Belle might not answer if she knows it's me, after all . . .

'Belle! Phone!' her mum yells. 'Make it quick.'

Yikes.

'Hello?' Belle says. Her voice sounds different. Quieter. Younger.

I take a deep breath, then talk really fast before she can hang up on me: 'Hi, Belle, it's Anni – I just wanted to say I'm really sorry, about lunchtime. I shouldn't have said all that stuff in front of everyone.'

'It's OK,' she says quickly. 'I'm really sorry too. Can I come over?'

'What?' I say, taken by surprise. I'd expected her to be furious. 'No, sorry – Granny's visiting.'

'That doesn't matter! I'll bring your mobile too, and—'

'No, Belle,' I say firmly. 'Bring it tomorrow.'

'Oh,' she says quietly. 'OK. B-but . . . we *are* BFFs again . . . aren't we?'

I falter. Her voice is so filled with pleading I hardly recognize it. But even so . . .

'I don't know.' I sigh. 'I'm not sure I want a BFF any more. Besides, we weren't really proper friends before, were we? Friends are meant to be there for each other, to support each other, not tell each other what to do.'

'I will! I mean, I won't! I *promise*!' Belle insists.

'Belle?' her mum's voice calls. 'Ask your friend if you can go over! Rick'll be here any minute.'

Who's Rick?

'Anni's busy.' Belle sighs.

'Well, what about one of your other friends?'

'I . . . um . . . just a minute, Mum!' Belle calls. 'Anni, I've got to go, but please, please, *please* walk to school with me tomorrow?'

I hesitate.

'*Please*, Anni!' she begs desperately. 'Just give me *one* more chance and I'll be the best friend you've ever had! I'll prove it to you! *Please!*'

Wow. What is going on? This isn't the cool, calm and confident Belle I know . . . But I guess everyone deserves a second chance – I've certainly learned that in the past few days.

'OK.'

'*Thank you!* See you tomorrow! Bye!' she says quickly.

But then I hear her mum's voice.

'What on earth are you wearing, girl? Your whole outfit looks like a charity-shop reject. I can't have Rick seeing you in that state – he'll never want you for a stepdaughter.'

I frown. Belle must've not hung up the phone properly.

'Come here and I'll fix your hair. How does it always

188

get into such a mess? And your skin's going all blotchy again. Have you been eating greasy food, young lady?'

'No, Mum! I had salad for lunch!' Belle protests.

'Well put some concealer on – what's the point in buying you all that make-up if you don't use it?'

'I do!'

'Well use *more*, then. Honestly, it's lucky you're clever, otherwise you'll never get a rich man like I've got Rick. How did you do in that test today? I hope you got full marks?'

I put the phone down, my heart heavy, my eyes opened.

Maybe Granny's right.

Maybe I didn't know Belle as well as I thought.

MAX

'That was delicious!' Dad cries as we finish dinner. 'Now, time for cake and prezzies!'

'Ooh, wait! I have to nip to the little girls' room first!' Granny says, hurrying out. 'Need to make some room!'

'*Mother!*' Mum gasps as I snort with laughter. Granny's been cracking us up all evening.

'Thanks so much for cooking, you two,' Dad says, smiling. 'And for tidying up earlier.'

'You've both been absolutely amazing,' Mum says, squeezing our hands. 'And on your birthday, too.'

Anni and I beam at each other, and she nods at me. *Now's the time.*

'Mum, Dad . . .' I clear my throat. 'We'd like to make an announcement.'

'Uh-oh, I knew it was too good to be true,' Dad groans, and Mum nudges him.

'Now we're older we'd like to help out more,' I continue.

'So we've drawn up a rota of chores,' Anni adds, pulling a piece of paper from her pocket. 'We're also both going to get paper rounds, so we'll be able to help out with money too.'

'Oh, sweethearts, you don't need to do that!' Mum cries.

'We want to,' Anni insists. 'We're thirteen now, after all.'

'And you should enjoy it,' Dad argues. 'You don't need to get a paper round for us, but if you want to, the money should be yours to spend as you like.'

'But we want to help!' I protest.

'You do already.' Mum smiles. 'You both brighten our lives every day.' She glances at Dad, who winks back. 'And speaking of announcements, we have one of our own.'

I smile at Anni, who's grinning like mad. *This is it!*

'You two have brought us so much joy, so much laughter and happiness –' Dad beams at Mum – 'that . . . we've decided to have another baby!'

'That's amazing!' I cry as Anni squeals, and we both jump up and rush to hug our parents.

'You don't mind?' Mum says anxiously.

'Of course not!' Anni laughs.

Dad raises an eyebrow. 'You don't seem very surprised?'

'We kind of worked it out.' I grin at Anni. 'And it's awesome. We'll even help babysit, and cook, and clean, and everything – except nappies!'

Dad bursts out laughing.

'Just be a loving big brother and sister,' Mum says with a smile, 'and this baby will be the luckiest child in the world.'

'Ooh, who's the luckiest child in the world?' Granny puffs, hurrying back into the room.

Mum smiles at her and squeezes Dad's hand. 'Our new baby, Mother. Raf and I are expecting another child.'

'A *baby*?' Granny's eyes widen, she takes a step forward – then suddenly collapses!

'*Mother!*' Mum jumps up, but I get to Granny first.

'She's not breathing!' I yell. 'Call an ambulance, quick!'

Dad pulls out his mobile, while I immediately start doing chest compressions.

'Max, what are you *doing*?' Mum shrieks, but I can't answer because I'm too busy singing 'Staying Alive' in my head.

'It's OK, Mum,' Anni says, hugging her. 'He knows what he's doing.'

I really, really hope she's right.

ANNI

So much for the perfect birthday, I think sadly as I lie in bed, listening for the telephone, or Mum and Dad coming back from the hospital. Instead I hear a knock on my bedroom door.

'Anni, are you awake?' Max whispers.

'Yes.' I sigh, as he creeps in and closes the door quietly so Nosy Nora downstairs won't hear. 'I'm too worried to sleep.'

'Me too,' he says, tiptoeing over and sitting beside me on my bed. 'I can't believe Mum wouldn't let us go with them to the hospital.'

'But they promised they'd let us know as soon as there's any news,' I reason, squeezing his hand. 'Besides, you already did the most important thing of all. You were amazing. The paramedics said your quick thinking probably saved Granny's life. There's nothing more we could do now, even if we were there.'

'True.' He sighs. 'But wait . . . Anni, there *is* something we can do! We can wish again!'

I freeze. 'Max . . . we can't.'

'Yes we can – we *have* to!' he insists. 'After all, Granny was only here because *I* suggested it – and it's *our* fault she got the shock of finding out that Mum's pregnant. If she'd stayed at home she'd be fine.'

My chest tightens. 'You don't know that.'

'It's true! This is the *only* thing that's gone wrong today. We can do everything else exactly the same tomorrow – we got everything else right!'

'I'm sorry, Max—'

'*Come on*, Anni – this is *Granny* we're talking about! Just one last time. *Please!*' he begs, squeezing my hand and breaking my heart.

I shake my head. 'I wish we could . . . but it's impossible.'

'Why?'

'Because . . . because I gave the candle away!' I confess.

Max stares at me, wide-eyed. 'You did WHAT?!' He snatches his hand from mine and storms around the room, hands in his hair. 'You . . . you had no *right*! That was *our* candle, Anni! How *could* you?!'

'I'm sorry!' I wail. 'I didn't know Granny would collapse. And Lottie needed it more than us. She needs a new heart! We're already so lucky, Max!'

'Yeah? I don't feel very lucky right now!'

'Come on, Max – we've had *four* chances to correct our mistakes, to save people from getting hurt and get things right!'

'But we could've had more!' Max says angrily.

'Yes, it could've *always* been our birthday, if you'd had your way!' I retort, exasperated. 'You kept wishing without me – I had to do *something*.'

He stops pacing and stares at me. 'No, I didn't.'

'What?'

'I've never wished without you. I've only ever wished on the candle twice – both times *with you*!'

'Really?' My stomach shifts uneasily. 'Promise?'

'*Promise!*'

He looks so upset, I believe him.

'But then . . .' My head spins. 'How have we had *four* repeated birthdays if we've only wished *twice*?'

'I've been thinking about that,' Max admits. 'Maybe each time we wished was a *double* wish – because we're twins?'

I frown. 'Maybe . . .'

'Or maybe we're being given the chance to redo the day over and over again until we get it right? Until we have the perfect birthday?' he says hopefully.

'I'm not sure there's really such a thing as a *perfect* birthday.' I sigh, hugging my knees. 'We'd be repeating today forever!'

'I s'pose,' Max says, miserably slumping on to my bed. 'I hope Lottie made the most of it.'

'She did.' I smile, remembering her ticking off her wish-list as she kept blowing out the candle. 'Omigosh!' I cry suddenly. 'That's *it*! The candle kept relighting itself!'

Max shrugs. 'So?'

'So we didn't make a new wish each time, did we? We

always wished to redo the day! Maybe *that's* why we've repeated our birthday so many times? Once for every time we blew it out!'

'Well how many was that?' Max asks anxiously.

'I don't know,' I wail. 'I can't remember!'

'Neither can I.' He frowns. 'But if you're right, it might be OK? Tomorrow might be today again anyway?'

'I think so.' I bite my lip. 'I *hope* so.'

'I hope so too.' Max's expression hardens. 'Because if it doesn't, and Granny dies because you gave our candle away, it'll be all your fault!'

'Max, don't say that!' I gasp, tears springing to my eyes.

'Why not?' he yells.

'That's . . . that's a *horrible* thing to say!'

'It's *true*!'

Suddenly the door flies open.

'Just what is going on in here?' Nora snaps. 'Max – back to bed this instant!'

'Fine,' he mutters, stomping past her.

'Straight to sleep, both of you,' Nora scolds.

But sleep is impossible. Because Max is right. It is all my fault. And there's nothing I can do to fix it.

DAY 6

MAX

As soon as I wake up, I sit up and sniff hard, hoping against hope to smell . . . bacon! *Yes!* Thank goodness! I flop back on my bed, flooded with relief as the salty smell fills my nostrils. It's our birthday again, which means Granny's OK!

Right, now all we need to do is replay yesterday, do everything exactly the same way, but *not* invite Granny for dinner. Maybe we can visit her at the weekend instead.

I hurry downstairs, ready to pick up my football kit – but it's not there. Weird. Maybe Anni got up earlier and moved it so I don't get into trouble? *Teamwork!*

'Morning, mate.' Dad smiles as I rush into the kitchen.

'Shall I help cook the bacon?' I say eagerly, trying to remember exactly what I said yesterday. 'I want to learn how to cook, and help out more.'

'Me too!' Anni cries, hurrying in behind me.

'That'd be great. Thanks, kids.' Dad ruffles my hair as he heads for the door. 'I'll try ringing your mum again.'

I freeze.

'Wh-why?' Anni says quietly. 'Where is she?'

Dad's smile falters. 'She's still at the hospital, love.'

The *hospital*? My heart crashes through the floor and

plummets all the way to Australia. For if Mum's at the hospital that must mean . . .

It's tomorrow.

ANNI

It's finally tomorrow. I can't believe it. The spell is broken, the loop has ended, Granny's in hospital, and Max isn't talking to me. He wouldn't even meet my gaze during breakfast, and barely touched his perfectly cooked bacon sandwich.

I take a deep breath and knock on his bedroom door. 'Max?'

To my surprise it opens immediately. 'Is there news about Granny?' Max asks anxiously.

'Um, no . . . Mum's still not answering her mobile, but—'

'Then go away, Anni!' He slams the door.

'Max, I'm so sorry, I didn't mean—'

'Just leave me alone!' he shouts through the door. 'I *hate* you!'

His words sting like a slap. But I can't blame him. I hate myself too. And I'd give anything to rewind the clock. How ironic is that?

'Anni!' Dad calls. 'Belle's here!'

I frown. *Belle?* I hurry downstairs and find her standing awkwardly on the doorstep.

'Hi!' She smiles hesitantly. 'Ready to walk to school?'

'I thought we were meeting at your house.' I frown, picking up my bag.

'I – I wasn't sure you'd come, after yesterday,' she stutters anxiously. 'And I really wanted to say sorry again, and . . . and congratulations!' She hands me a card.

I blink. 'For what?'

'For getting cast in the school musical, of course!'

'*What?*'

'Didn't you know?' Belle laughs as we walk down the road. 'The list was up after school yesterday. You're Nessarose! I'm so pleased for you, Anni – you totally deserve it.'

Excitement ripples through me. *I actually got a part?* And Belle's *pleased* for me, even though this is just the sort of thing that broke her and Freya up! I smile at the card, which has a hand-drawn picture of me standing on a stage, and suddenly remember the one Belle made me when I was off school.

'Here.' She passes me my mobile phone. 'Thanks so much for lending it to me, and I'm really sorry I kept forgetting to give it back – but I've downloaded the whole soundtrack to *Wicked* on to it so you can practise. Happy belated birthday!' She smiles nervously.

'Thanks, Belle – that's really thoughtful.' I smile back. 'I can't wait to listen to it!'

Her smile falters. 'Unfortunately, all that downloading kind of used up the battery, and I didn't have the right charger – I'm really, really sorry!'

'That's OK. Thanks, Belle.' Maybe she *does* care about me after all? Maybe Granny was right, and she's just insecure?

Granny.

Guilt crashes down on top of me and smashes my happiness into smithereens.

'What's the matter?' Belle frowns. 'I thought you'd be celebrating.'

'I don't really feel like it,' I mumble.

'Why not?'

'My granny's in hospital. She collapsed last night.' *And it's all my fault*, I add silently.

'Oh no!' Belle stops dead. 'Oh my gosh, Anni; I'm so sorry!' She startles me by pulling me into a tight hug. She's never hugged me before, not properly. 'You must be so worried. Grandparents are so special.' Her voice cracks.

'Are you OK?' I ask gently. I've never seen Belle cry before. 'Are you close to your grandparents?'

She nods, then smiles weakly, her eyes watery. 'My gran brought me up.'

'Really?' I frown, realizing there's an awful lot I don't know about her. 'How come?'

'Mum was always away – she used to be an air hostess – so most of the time it was just me and Gran.' Her eyes brighten. 'She was the kindest person I've ever known. We had so much fun together, and she gave the best hugs . . .' Belle's bottom lip trembles. 'But she . . . she died a couple of years ago. I still miss her every day.'

'I'm so sorry, Belle,' I say, putting my arm around her.

'Gosh, Anni, you shouldn't be comforting *me* – *you're* the one whose granny's ill.' Belle sniffs, tears spilling over her lashes as she blinks furiously. 'You were right. I always have to be the centre of attention . . . I don't know what's wrong with me.'

'Shh.' I pass her a tissue from my pocket. 'It's OK.'

'And I can't believe I'm *crying*! Ugh! How *lame*!'

I laugh. '*Lame?*'

'Crying shows weakness.'

'Says who?'

'Mum.' Belle sniffs, and suddenly everything falls into place. I remember how critical Belle's mum was when I overheard her on the phone last night, and how keen she was for Belle to go out . . . *That's* why Belle's always at my house and never invites me to hers. It's not because she's embarrassed by me. Maybe that's even why she lied about her test result? Was her offer to help me study just another excuse to come round – to *sleep over*, even? Does she *always* feel she's in her mum's way? That's so sad, and so different to my mum and dad, who try to spend as much time as possible with us – sometimes *too* much. Poor Belle. Suddenly her behaviour is a lot more understandable. And forgivable.

'Ugh, now my mascara's running!' Belle wails. 'And I bet my eyes have gone all yucky and puffy too!'

'OK, firstly, you don't need mascara,' I tell her firmly. 'You don't need *any* make-up, Belle. You're already beautiful. Plus, it gives you spots – how ironic is that? Besides, make-up's for old ladies trying to look younger.'

She laughs shakily.

'Secondly, crying isn't *lame*, and it doesn't show *weakness* either. It's honest, and it's real. And that's much more important than being *cool*.'

'You think so?' She sniffs.

'Belle, you never have to hide your feelings – not from me. I don't care if your eyes are puffy. We all cry. Besides, that's the best thing about having friends.' I smile, squeezing her arm. 'You can be totally yourself. Otherwise, what's the point, right?'

A slow smile spreads across Belle's face, and she squeezes me back. 'Right.'

MAX

'Are you OK?' Ben asks me for the millionth time at lunch. 'You've hardly touched your food.'

'I'm not hungry.'

He frowns. 'But you're always hungry . . .'

'Cheer up, lads!' Jamie calls from across the table. 'We won the Cup – and it's *Friday*!'

Friday. My heart sinks. It's usually my favourite day – the start of the weekend – but not today. Today I'd give anything to rewind the clock.

'Do you want to talk about it?' Ben asks gently. 'It might help. My mum says a problem shared is a problem halved.'

'Thanks, mate, but no.' I sigh. I *can't* talk about it, and besides, it won't help.

Only one thing would. And thanks to Anni, it's too late for that.

Because it's Friday.

Suddenly I hear the unmistakable ringtone of a mobile phone.

'Is that your phone, Ben?' I frown.

'No, my phone's at home.' Ben shrugs, looking around. 'It sounds like it's coming from your bag . . .'

He's right. Hurriedly I unzip my backpack and search through my books, till I find Mrs MacCready's mobile! I forgot I still had it! Whoever's calling might know if she's OK! I quickly put the phone on silent, then hurry to the loos to answer it, leaving Ben and my uneaten lunch behind.

'Hello?'

'Are you Max?' a man's voice says. 'The lad who rang

Brendan yesterday when my mother – Mrs MacCready – was rushed to hospital?'

'Yes!' I say quickly. 'How is she? Is she OK?'

'She's doing really well, thanks mostly to you, I understand,' he says. 'They say you saved her life.'

'Thank goodness!' I beam, filled with relief.

'Thanks so much for calling Brendan too. What's your address? I'll pop round and collect Mum's mobile from you.'

'Oh, I'll drop it round if you like,' I offer. 'I pass her house on my way home from school.'

'Actually, Mum won't be living there any more,' he explains. 'She's going to come and stay with us instead so we can look after her.'

I smile, thinking of how lonely she'd seemed when we had that hot chocolate together. 'She'll really like that.'

'So will we. I can't believe we nearly lost her – can't believe I hadn't seen her in so long.' He swallows hard. 'Don't hold grudges, Max, that's my advice. Life's too short.'

I give him my address, then hang up, a warm feeling spreading through me. Mrs MacCready's OK, she's going to be looked after, and she's going to live with the family she missed so much.

Friday's finally looking up.

ANNI

'Hm, what's for lunch?' Belle says, scanning the lunch

counter. 'Fish and chips or . . . vegetable stew.'

'Fish and chips, please,' I say, though I'm so worried about Granny I'm not very hungry.

'Really?' Belle says and my heart sinks. She's going to judge me *again*? Just when I thought she'd changed . . .

'Snap! That's what I'm going to have.' She grins and I smile, relieved. Today's actually gone really well so far, Belle-wise. She hasn't put me down once, hasn't been mean to anyone, and she's seemed so much calmer somehow.

'Hi, Anni!' Freya says, stopping by our table. 'Don't forget we've got our first rehearsal after school. I can't wait!'

'See you there!' I reply. But if it wasn't the very first rehearsal, I probably wouldn't go. I don't really feel like singing today, not when Granny's in hospital.

'You and Freya are friends now, huh?' Belle says quietly, picking at her chips.

'I'm just getting to know her.' I shrug. 'But she seems really nice.'

'She is.' Belle sighs. 'I'm just worried she'll turn you against me. She hates me.'

'She doesn't *hate* you,' I reason. 'She was just hurt when you suddenly stopped being friends.'

'But *she* ditched *me*!' Belle protests. 'One minute we were BFFs, the next she'd dumped me to join the choir, leaving me all by myself. Everyone else was already in groups. It was awful.'

I frown. I know exactly how that feels.

'That's not what Freya says,' I argue. 'She thought you guys would make up, but then you replaced her. With me.'

Belle's jaw drops. 'But I thought *she* didn't want to be *my* friend any more. She started wearing her earphones and hanging out by herself and looked perfectly happy. It was like she was telling everyone she'd rather be alone than be friends with me. And there's *nothing* worse than being alone.'

'How about being called Freaky Freya? That was mean, Belle.'

'But she made up *my* nickname!' Belle argues. 'At least, I assume she did.'

'What nickname?' I frown.

She shifts uncomfortably. 'Dumb-Belle.'

I burst out laughing. I'd forgotten Idris called her that at my disastrous party.

'Now who's mean, Anni?' Belle mutters.

'I'm only laughing because that's such a *dumb* nickname!' I explain. 'You're one of the cleverest girls in the year – how can you possibly be offended by it?'

Belle smiles slowly. 'I s'pose . . .'

'You know what? I think we both need to make more

friends.' I stand up and pick up my lunch-tray.

Belle looks up anxiously. 'You're ditching me too?'

'No.' I smile. 'But I'm going to have musical rehearsals during lunchtimes from now on. What are you going to do?'

'I don't know. Sit in the library? Buy some earphones?'

'Come on.' I head towards a table of Year 8 girls. 'We're going to make new friends.' I smile. 'Together.'

MAX

'Anni!' I run after her as she hurries home from rehearsals.

'Max.' She looks round startled. 'H-how was football?'

'Fine. Have you heard any news? About Granny?'

She shakes her head. 'Belle lent me her mobile, but Mum and Dad didn't answer. You?'

'No.' I sigh. I tried calling them on Mrs MacCready's phone but there was no response. 'But they probably didn't recognize the number – and they have to keep their phones off in the hospital, right? They'd have called the school if . . . if there was bad news.'

Anni nods miserably. 'Max, I'm so, so sorry—'

'No, Anni, *I'm* sorry,' I interrupt. 'I should never have blamed you. Whatever happens to Granny . . . it's not your fault.' After all, Mr MacCready's right. Life's too short for grudges. 'You could never have known what would happen.'

'I wish I had,' she says sadly.

'We can't ever know *all* the consequences of our actions. Even if it was yesterday again, and we tried to *save* Granny, there'd be *new* consequences.'

'The butterfly effect.' Anni nods.

'And I think it's true what you said, that there's no such thing as the perfect day. Although we came pretty close yesterday.' I smile. 'Mrs MacCready's son called me. She's going to be OK, and she's going to go and live with her family once she's out of hospital.'

'That's wonderful!' Anni cries. 'And you saved the little girls *and* won the Cup.'

'You did a lot of good too,' I remind her. 'If it wasn't for you, we wouldn't know that Mum's pregnant and she'd still be stressed out about it.'

Anni nods. 'But it's also *my* fault Granny's in hospital,' she says, her voice cracking.

'*Our* fault,' I correct, hugging her. 'It was my idea to invite her over.'

'But *I* gave away our candle – just when we need it most!' Anni sobs. 'It's so unfair. We had this power to rewrite history, to make things better, but now our granny's in danger, we're helpless. I'm so sorry, Max.'

'Hey, I told you, it's not your fault,' I soothe. 'Besides, maybe Granny'll be OK. After all, she's got more spirit than Dad's entire secret store of whisky.'

'And more bottle!' Anni giggles.

'Yeah.' I smile. 'So let's get home and see if there's any news, eh?'

But as we hurry up our street, Nosy Nora rushes out of her house.

'There you are!' she cries. 'At last!'

'Has something happened?' I ask quickly. 'How's Granny?'

'I don't know!' she says briskly. 'Your mum called and asked me to take you to the supermarket.'

I frown. 'The *supermarket*?'

'She must still be at the hospital,' Anni says anxiously. 'Is there bad news? Is that why we're being kept out of the way? How did Mum seem?'

'She seemed perfectly fine. Your dad'll be back later, and she wants the shopping done before then, so it's one less thing to worry about,' Nora snaps. 'I thought you two wanted to help out more?'

'We do,' I say. 'But—'

'Then *come on*!' she cries, bustling us into her car. 'I haven't got all day!'

ANNI

Omigosh, Nora is like a sergeant major on a mission! She keeps sending us off to compare prices on everything on her endless list in all different parts of the *enormous* supermarket – we must have trekked for *miles* down the aisles!

Finally, wearily, we push the heaving trolley towards the exit.

'Wait – I need coffee!' Nora barks, striding towards the cafe. 'I'm exhausted!'

I look at Max. *She's* exhausted? We did all the work!

'I'll make you one at home!' I offer, glancing at my watch.

'I can't possibly drive all that way without caffeine! Come on!'

'Can I at least fetch my bag from your car?' Max begs. 'Or borrow your mobile to call Dad?'

'*No!*' Nora snaps, joining the giant queue. 'You'll be home in ten minutes – don't be so impatient!'

But ten minutes turn into forty as Max and I restlessly watch Nora take tiny sips from the biggest coffee I've ever seen – seriously, it's more like a *bowl* than a cup – then takes so long in the loos afterwards, I'm sincerely worried about her health.

If only my mobile wasn't dead – or I had any change for the payphone . . .

Finally we get back in the car and head home.

'Still no answer.' Max frowns, trying Mrs MacCready's mobile again. 'Dad *must* be home by now?'

But the lights in our house are all off as we pull up outside.

Uh-oh. Where are they?

We hurry inside and flick on the lights.

'*SURPRISE!*'

I stumble backwards into Max as dozens of people jump out singing 'Happy birthday!'

No, no, NO! I panic, feeling sick with déjà vu. I thought this nightmare was over – has Belle done it *again?* I look around. There she is, with Freya, and practically everyone from the *Wicked* cast, and all of Max's football team, clapping along as they sing. We're going to be in SO much trouble – this is the *last* thing Mum and Dad need at the moment. None of us are exactly in a celebratory mood, and it's not even our birthday any more – *finally*!

'Happy birthday, lovely twins!' Nora cries, appearing behind us and ruffling our hair. 'I know you didn't exactly have a very happy birthday yesterday, so your parents thought this would cheer you up.'

What? Mum and Dad organized this? I search the crowd and spot Dad by the kitchen door, smiling at us.

'Happy belated birthday!' Belle cries, hugging me. 'Are you surprised?'

'Very!' I nod. 'How did this even happen?'

'Your mum called me after school,' she explains. 'She asked me to invite all your friends over, so I asked the girls in our class, then called Freya, and she told everyone in *Wicked*. Lucky I still have her number.' She smiles. 'Your mum said your neighbour would keep you busy till everything was ready.'

So *that's* what the epic shopping trip was about!

'But it's not even our birthday any more!' I say, confused.

'No, it's your *un*-birthday,' a voice says, and I turn to see George smiling at me. My stomach flip-flops. George knows who I am? George is at my party? George is *smiling* at me?

'I hear you visited my sister yesterday.' He grins, his blue eyes sparkling.

I frown. 'Your sister?'

'Lottie.'

I gasp. '*You're* Lottie's brother?'

He nods. 'I knew it must have been you from the way she described you. It was so kind what you did for her, you really made her day.'

'Oh, well, she made mine.' I smile, feeling my cheeks flush. 'She's so lovely. How is she doing?'

'Really well. She won't stop singing, though. She knows all the *Wicked* songs already!'

I laugh. 'Maybe she can help me learn them! I thought I might visit her over the weekend if . . . if that's OK?'

'Of course it's OK!' George smiles. 'Actually, I'm going tomorrow afternoon, if you'd like to go together?'

I beam. 'That'd be . . . wicked!'

MAX

'Happy birthday, Max!' Ben cries, and the entire football team lunge at me, patting my back and ruffling my hair.

'Ben, you kept this quiet *all day*?' I laugh, amazed.

'I didn't *know*!' he confesses. 'Your mum called our parents and asked them to bring us straight here after football!'

Mum did?

'Hi, you must be Max.' A boy I don't know hurries up to me with a middle-aged man. 'I'm Brendan. This is my dad.'

'Hi!' I recognize him now from Mrs MacCready's photos. 'You've come to collect the phone.' I shrug off my school bag.

'No rush,' Mr MacCready says, smiling. 'We're here because we wanted to thank you in person for what you did.'

I shrug. 'Anyone would've done the same.'

'I wish that were true,' a man behind me says. 'I'm afraid I didn't have a clue what to do.'

I turn, surprised. 'Mr Smith? What are you doing here?'

'Please, call me John,' he says. 'I've come to say thank you too, lad. You not only saved Mrs MacCready yesterday, I think you probably saved me too. I had no idea how dangerous driving while using my phone could be. I'm so terribly sorry.'

'What's going to happen to you?' I ask tentatively. 'With the police, I mean?'

'Mrs MacCready's asked the police for leniency, so they say I might just get a fine.' John shakes his head. 'I don't know why she was so forgiving. I deserve to go to jail. I was so stupid. It could've been so much worse.'

I think back on the last few days. *Yes, it could.*

'I'd give anything to rewind the clock.' John sighs, and I swallow hard, realizing just how lucky I've been the past few 'todays'. It's easy to judge, but not everyone gets the chance to rectify their mistakes like I have.

Mr MacCready pats John on the shoulder. 'Everyone makes mistakes. It's learning from them that counts – that's what Mum always says.'

'And I have,' John promises. 'I'm going to make it my mission to make sure as many people as possible know the risks.' He looks at me. 'And learn CPR, of course. I had a word with your Headmaster about that, Max.'

'Mr Peters?' I blink. 'But how did you know where I go to school? And where I live?'

He smiles. 'You were wearing your Bridgehill School uniform yesterday, and I overheard you tell the dispatcher your name, so I called your school this morning and thanked them for teaching CPR – and they said they don't! Well, that's going to change, believe me. They gave me your mum's phone number and I called her to ask if I could come over to thank you – but she didn't seem to know anything about what had happened!'

'Oh, well, it was nothing.' I shrug, my cheeks growing warm.

'Hardly!' Brendan laughs. 'It's not every day you save someone's life – especially on your birthday!'

'*Two* lives,' John corrects.

'Make that three,' Dad says, and I turn to see him smiling at me.

'*Three* lives?' I say, my heart lifting. 'You mean –'

'Granny's all right?' Anni hurries over. 'Really?'

'She will be.' Dad smiles. 'Thanks to Max. The doctors said the heart attack could have happened at any time and that if Max hadn't responded so quickly, it would have been a very different story. It seems she's got a slight heart problem.'

'What?' Anni gasps.

'Nothing major,' Dad says quickly. 'Don't look so worried. They can treat it with the right medication, and she's started the tablets already. But if she hadn't had that mild attack, the problem would have just kept on getting worse until she had a major one.'

'So it's actually *good* that she had a mild heart attack?' Anni asks.

Dad laughs. 'Strange as it sounds, it probably saved her life. That and the fact that you were here and knew what to do, Max. I just thank my lucky stars you suggested inviting Granny over yesterday.'

'Me too.' Anni nods.

I stare at them, dazed. But if I'd had my way and we'd managed to redo today again, I *wouldn't* have invited Granny over . . . Thank goodness we *didn't* get to make another wish!

'So Mum and I felt a multiple celebration was in order!' Dad announces. 'It's a belated birthday party, first and foremost, but it's also a big congratulations to Anni, and everyone who got cast in the school musical!'

Anni beams as the rest of the cast cheers.

'And congratulations to Max for being a hero. We're so proud of you.'

I feel my cheeks burn as everyone claps.

'And to Bridgehill School football team for winning the Cup!'

I whoop along with the rest of the team – the rowdiest bunch of all.

'And congratulations to you and Mum, too,' Anni pipes up. 'We can't wait to meet our new little brother or sister.'

'Or both!' I cry, and everyone laughs.

'I just wish Mum and Granny were here to celebrate with us,' Anni says.

'Your wish is my command!' Dad laughs, pulling out his mobile, pressing speed-dial, then passing it to us.

'Hi, everyone!' Mum grins at us from the screen. 'Happy belated birthday party!'

'Thanks, Mum!' I cry. 'How's Granny?'

'Why don't you ask her yourself?' She smiles, passing the phone to Granny, who's lying in a hospital bed.

'Hello, darlings.' She smiles weakly, looking pale but so much better than the last time I saw her. 'Sorry about last night – very rude of me to ruin your birthday.'

'Don't be silly!' Anni says. 'How are you feeling?'

'Oh I'll be right as rain in no time. I'm just miffed I'm missing your party – it looks like fun.'

'We'll have another one when you're out,' I promise.

'About that,' Mum says, taking the phone and hurrying away from Granny's bed. My heart beats faster. *What's wrong? Won't she be coming out of hospital?*

'Granny's going to need a bit of looking after when she comes out, so—'

'Why doesn't she move in with us?' I interrupt.

Mum smiles. 'That's just what Dad and I were going to suggest, but we wanted to ask you two first. We know there's a lot of changes happening at the moment.'

'It's fine, really!' I insist. 'Isn't it, Anni?'

'Better than fine! It'd be brilliant!' Anni cries.

'Great!' Mum beams. 'We thought you two might like to ask her yourselves.' She passes the phone back to Granny.

'What was all that whispering about?' She frowns.

'What mischief are you up to?'

'No mischief,' I say with a grin. 'Granny, would you like to come and live with us?'

Her wrinkled face slowly lights up into the most beautiful smile and suddenly she looks ten years younger. 'Really? That'd be *wonderful*!'

Anni and I beam at each other, and Dad grins at us both.

'I can help look after the baby,' Granny continues excitedly. 'That way Felicity can still work if she wants to, and my house should fetch a good price too, big old thing. That'll help buy a few nappies!'

'Mother,' I hear Mum say. 'We don't need you to babysit, and we don't need your money. We'd just like to spend more time with you.'

'Tush!' Granny laughs. 'I love babies, you know that! Besides what else am I going to do with all my money?'

'We'll talk about this later, OK?' Mum smiles. 'You just concentrate on getting better.'

'Pah! I'll be out in no time!' I hear Granny laugh. 'See you soon, twins!'

I grin at Anni. This has all worked out better than we could have ever hoped!

'You know what?' she says, nudging me. 'I think I was wrong and you were right.'

'*What?* Did I hear correctly? You, Anni, my twin sister, admit you were *wrong* about something?'

She rolls her eyes, then smiles. 'I think there *is* such a thing as the perfect day.'

I follow her gaze round the room and smile as I see Brendan patting John's shoulder, Ben re-enacting his match-winning goal, and Belle laughing with Anni's musical friends.

Anni seems so much more relaxed too. It's like she's finally grown into herself. She's not hiding away or worrying, and actually seems . . . confident. Best of all, Granny's going to be OK, and all Mum and Dad's baby worries have just fluttered out the window.

'Well, *duh*!' I scoff, ruffling Anni's hair. 'I'm *always* right!'

'I wouldn't go that far!' She laughs, hooking my arm. 'But this time, I couldn't be happier.'